MW01264310

Michael Schneider

To Duanna,

Love
Michael Schneider

Blind Faith

The Writer's Coffee Shop
Publishing House

First published by The Writer's Coffee Shop, 2010

Copyright © Michael Schneider, 2010

The right of Michael Schneider to be identified and the author of this work has been asserted by her under the *Copyright Amendment (Moral Rights) Act 2000*

This work is copyright. Apart from any use as permitted under the Copyright Act 1968, no part maybe reproduced, copied, scanned, stored in a retrieval system, recorded or transmitted, in any form or by any means, without the prior written permission of the publisher.

This book is a work of fiction. Names, characters, places and incidents are either a product of the author's imagination or are used fictitiously. Any resemblance to actual people living or dead, events or locales is entirely coincidental.

The Writer's Coffee Shop
(Australia)   PO Box 2013 Hornsby Westfield NSW 1635
(USA)   PO Box 2116 Waxahachie TX 75168

Paperback ISBN-13: 9871612130026
E-book ISBN-13: 9781612130033

A CIP catalogue record for this book is available from the US Congress Library.

Cover image by: Bowie15
Cover design by: Jennifer McGuire

www.thewriterscoffeeshop.com/mschneider

Michael Schneider came to find her passion for writing in an unconventional way. Her daughter, after reading a story online, dared her to create an online work of fiction worth reading. Having always been a bit creative, and not one to back down from any challenge her children posed, Michael accepted the dare and discovered an enthusiasm for writing. With the encouragement of family and friends, her passion blossomed from a fun hobby into a published work. Though the challenges of raising children often produces mixed emotions, Michael is truly grateful to her daughter for this particular challenge.

Michael, the mother of three girls, has been married to her high school sweetheart for 27 years. A central Texas native, Michael lives in a small town outside of Austin with her husband, teenage daughter and two cats. When she is not busy writing, or balancing the role of wife and mother, Michael can usually be found quilting or gardening. She also enjoys watching science fiction movies and visiting area antique stores with her friends and family.

If Karsyn McKenna is guilty of anything, it's longing for love, finding herself surrounded by men whose main concern is their own self-interest, and maybe, possibly not asking questions. But that is what blind faith is, having unconditional trust in those who are supposed to give of themselves unconditionally and without false pretense.

Blind Faith by Michael Schneider, propels the reader into a quick-paced journey of tangled webs of omission and deception shrouded by a cloud of innocent acceptance. Armed with nothing except the truth she has been presented, Karsyn is unwittingly coerced to dive head first into a cave so deep, that the only thing that can rescue her is the courage she must find deep within. Readers will take the journey with her from naïve shop owner's daughter to potential WITSEC candidate in just a couple short years.

Like every good story, a ride of emotions is waiting for the reader. Frustration is apparent as you will silently beg her to "*live life with both eyes open*" and see what is in front of her, as if you can send brain waves to carry your message. But that's not all, don't be alarmed if you find yourself torn between which ending would better suit Karsyn by the end; there are definitely points where you can see the pros and cons of each path, which only she can ultimately choose.

Despite what she has been through, Karsyn is able to rise out of the ashes, happy and victorious, ultimately finding her place right where she was meant to be. When all is said and done and the dust from the firearms settles, her blind faith is what leads her to the golden path of a life worth living.

Nai - The Review Lounge.

Dedicated To

To my wonderful husband of twenty-seven years. Thank you for the pots of coffee and fresh glasses of iced tea while I neglected all things domestic to make this a reality. You really are the very best and I'll love you forever. Thank you for believing in me.

To my beautiful girls; Caitlin, Rachael, Meagan and Katie. Thank you for daring me to take a chance. Thank you for all the laughter and not being embarrassed by the things your momma says and does. I truly thank you for the friendship we have developed that goes so far beyond just mother and daughter. Y'all will always be my greatest accomplishments.

To my amazing friend, Mandy who dragged me kicking and screaming into the 21st century. Thank you for creating a welcoming environment that gives writers a chance to test their wings. We soar because of you. Thanks also to your wonderful family for sharing you with us.

To Janine. There aren't enough words in the English language to thank you for everything you do. But I know if I found them you'd put all the commas in place and make them shine. Thank you for putting up with me.

And last but not least, my undying gratitude to my pre-readers; Jenny, Jo, Pat and Michelle. Thank you so much for reassuring me along the way, that I could do this and telling me when I've screwed up.

Prologue

September 5, 2009

I brushed the tinted gloss on my lips and sprayed perfume on my pulse points before stepping back to give myself a last once over. Today was a special day, and I needed him to be pleased. The white halter dress I wore showed off my dark tan and fell in gentle folds to my ankles. My feet were bare, but I had no need for shoes. I spent most of my time barefoot, anyway, unless I took a walk on the beach when the sand was too hot.

My strawberry blonde hair was streaked from the sun and so much lighter than it used to be. Soft curls surrounded my face and fell down my back. A prickling of perspiration trailed down the back of my neck, and I lifted my heavy locks for a moment of relief before letting them fall again. I was so wrong to cut my hair in a fit of anger. It was finally growing back. He would be happy, and that's all that mattered to me now.

I slipped the large diamond-stud earrings in my ears and wrapped the diamond tennis bracelet around my wrist—both presents from my husband. I swallowed the sudden lump in my throat and took a shuddering breath. I closed my eyes against the memories. Not yet.

I took the hanger off the bathroom door and walked back into the bedroom to lay my satin nightgown across the bed for later tonight. It had arrived last week along with everything I had requested. He often included surprises like this; a new dress, lingerie, a music box, some trinket to remind me I was always in his thoughts—as if there was ever any doubt.

His favorite brandy and a glass were on the bedside table. I spared a brief glance at the upper corner of the ceiling as I surveyed the room. Everything was as perfect as it was going to get. I'd spent the last couple of days preparing and knew the downstairs was ready. Dinner was in the refrigerator, and I would only need to put the tray in the oven to heat when the time came. The dining table was set, and pink streamers hung from the chandelier for this evening.

There was nothing left to do but wait and think, and thinking never boded well for me. Too much time with my thoughts usually upset me and left me wishing things had turned out different. Sometimes, though, I needed those memories. I used them to play out the scenes differently than how real life had turned out. I could write my own happy ending to help me through the days and nights. Today was one of those days.

I stepped onto the balcony outside my bedroom, sank into the wicker loveseat, and stared at the view I'd come to know so well while absently twisting my wedding ring around my finger. To anyone else the view was breathtaking, and in another life, I would have agreed. I used to love the ocean, but no longer. I closed my eyes, listened to the sounds of the tide lapping at the sand on the nearby beach, and inhaled the salty air as the breeze brushed softly against my skin. I tried to find peace in my surroundings. Sighing, I opened my eyes after a few minutes and stared out at the water, unsuccessful at finding any peace. I knew the yacht was out there in the distance, coming closer with each passing moment. It was still too far away for me to see. On that yacht was my greatest joy and also my greatest misery.

I had enough time for a stroll down memory lane to help fortify me for the days ahead. I reminisced about all the good things and hoped to keep all the bad at bay just for the next three days. So many things I would have done differently if only I hadn't denied what was in front of my eyes.

There were so many "if onlys" in my life. If only I had listened to the stories instead of making excuses. If only I had given my trust when I gave my heart instead of withholding it for one undeserving. If only I had trusted my instincts when faced with the evidence. If only I had told my husband that, my best friend and I changed our plans instead of wanting to surprise him.

My locket always hung around my neck. Grasping it in a tight fist, I closed my eyes and let the painful memories wash over me again.

Chapter One

June 2007

I tried to ignore the catcalls of the men working the construction site across the street, refusing to look their way as I fought to pull the spare tire out of the trunk of my car. What a sight I must have made in my short navy dress as I bent over the inside of my trunk. I kept tugging at the back hem, making sure my butt was covered at all times. Sniffing at the tears of frustration, which threatened to spill, and swallowing hard, I tugged again at the tire, wanting to scream because it wouldn't budge from the floor of the trunk.

I didn't want to call my dad to come help, or I'd get stuck listening to him lecture me. I could just hear him. "If you're old enough to drive, you're old enough to change a tire." Unfortunately, I didn't pay attention when he taught me back when I first started driving, so now I was paying the price.

"Please, just come on. Give me a freaking break," my voice steadily rose as I screeched at the tire, wishing it would just listen and jump out of the trunk for me. Magically changing itself would be a nice touch too. The urge to stomp my high heeled foot was so strong; I actually had to make a conscious effort to keep both feet firmly planted on the ground.

"Looks like you could use some help." A deep voice chuckled near my ear as a hand patted my backside.

I jumped up, slamming the top of my head into someone's hard chin. I heard a grunt as I spun around, ready to defend myself. Relief washed over me as I realized who it was.

"Oh, Chase, I'm so sorry!" My hands fluttered around not knowing if I should rub his chin or hug him. My eyes narrowed instead. "You scared me," I accused. I settled for punching his chest with my small fist.

He laughed at me, rubbing his chin. "You should stick to hitting with your head, Karsyn. It hurts more than your puny fist. Now move that cute little butt of yours out of my way so I can change your tire."

He playfully nudged me to the side with his hip and reached into the trunk to take out the spare. I flushed in embarrassment as he spun the nut in the center of the rim, unscrewing it from the base before pulling the tire out.

"I didn't know it was screwed down," I mumbled my excuse.

"What? Didn't Daddy teach you how to change a tire? I would think the daughter of a mechanic would be able to change a tire in her sleep," he said, laughing at me.

I sighed in resignation, knowing I was going to disappointment my father when he found out I couldn't change the tire. Over the years, he tried, unsuccessfully, to teach me how to care for a car, but I was never that interested. My father, Carson McKenna, had wanted a son, a junior, someone to go hunting and fishing with, someone to work side-by-side with in his garage. He envisioned a younger version of himself to drink beer and shoot pool with, to be able to play the proud father at football games.

Instead, he got me, Karsyn, not quite the junior he'd hoped for. No, I was as far from his dream child as you could get. Slender at 5' 6" and 115 lbs, I was all girl. My emerald green eyes were the only thing I inherited from my dad. I hated the idea of shooting Bambi; fishing was boring, and the garage was greasy and dirty. I credited my grandmother with ensuring I knew how to be a lady instead of a female version of Dad. Mom died when I was born, and Gran moved in to help take care of me until she passed away three years ago. She helped bridge the gap between us, and despite his disappointment in not having a son, I became Daddy's little girl. I had ballet and piano lessons. He did get to go to all the football games like he dreamed; only it was to watch me cheer for the team instead.

"Just shut up, Chase. I would think the son of the richest man in the county wouldn't know how to change a tire. Don't you have people for that? I guess we were both wrong," I teased, crossing my arms over my chest.

Chase Carter was the son of Chester Carter III and every girl's dream. He was 6' 4" with broad shoulders, thick brown hair, and crystal blue eyes. Since his father's stroke last winter, he took over running his family's business interests. Their company was headquartered in Longview, fifty miles away. His mother passed away from cancer while he was still in college. At twenty-four, Chase was six years older than me. We became friends when I was fourteen. He'd come to my father's garage to get the oil changed in his truck and found me down on the ground with my arm stuck behind the soda machine, trying to reach a stray kitten. He helped me get the kitten out, earning several scratches and a bite on his finger, which became infected. He'd been my hero ever since, always managing to come to my rescue when I needed him. Despite our age difference, he was one of my best friends.

His great-great grandfather founded our town back in the 1800's after striking it rich in the California gold rush. He moved his family to Texas and bought up a hefty chunk of East Texas to settle. His Midas touch struck again when large deposits of oil were found on his property. He built the town around them to support the workers and their families. Naturally, there were the usual whispers that followed anyone who had more than the average person, insinuating not everything the Carters owned had been obtained on the up and up. Occasionally a rumor would circulate that someone had left town in fear for their life or that some random act of violence was actually retaliation for crossing Chase or his father.

My father constantly told me to ignore the gossip; people were just petty and jealous. Mr. Carter had always treated us well. Instead of taking their personal and company vehicles to one of those larger, well-known garages in the city to handle the maintenance for a better price, the Carters gave the contract to my dad and renewed it every year. Even their employees came to my dad. Mr. Carter sponsored me through high school anytime I had a fundraiser for cheerleading camps or uniforms. He invited my dad fishing in the summers and hunting on his deer lease in the winter.

I sat on the curb waiting while Chase changed my flat. It only took a few minutes for him to finish, toss the flat tire in the trunk, and slam the top closed. He brushed his dirty hands on his jeans and walked over to me.

"That should get you home until your dad can fix your tire." He reached down to take my hands and pulled me up. I stood and turned to pick up my magazine I had been sitting on to keep my dress from getting dirty. "So what are you up to today?" he asked as he checked over my attire.

I huffed. "I'm looking for a job. Daddy's been having trouble with his back again, so I want to help out, but no one is hiring in town. I'm going to start searching in the city next," I explained.

"Well, I was headed to the Double S for a piece of pecan pie. I've got some business with Scott. Come keep me company," he offered as he eyed me thoughtfully.

"Sure, why not?" I replied, looking down at my dirty hands. I wouldn't be doing any more job hunting today anyway.

We crossed the street to the restaurant. The construction crew that had been yelling lewd comments at me earlier was now working diligently on the restaurant's expansion. It didn't hurt that the owner of the construction company happened to be walking beside me.

"My hero." I smirked as we passed them by.

Chase opened the door for me and winked in return. "But of course. Every girl needs a personal Superman. I'm yours."

Chapter Two

Chase ushered me into the restaurant. There were only a couple of places to eat in town, the Double S Steakhouse and La Familia Mexican restaurant down the street.

Double S was owned by Scott and Sandy Wilson. Scott had been a chef at a five star restaurant in New York and now shared his talents with our small town. He and his wife moved here about ten years ago, wanting a quieter place to live and start a family. They had seven-year-old twin girls, Dena and Dana, who I babysat until I graduated high school a month ago. The job was a great source of spending money.

Chase led me to a booth in the back corner where he liked to sit. He left to wash his hands before coming back and sliding in beside me. He draped his arm over the back of the booth and began absently twisting my hair around his finger while he gestured for the waitress. She hurried over to us, grabbing a couple of menus on the way.

"Hey, Chase. What can I get for you today?" she asked with a wink and a smile. Her gaze fell on me, and she eyed me snidely. "Hello, Karsyn, what are you doing here? Is high school out already for the summer?"

"Hi, Brandi," I replied stiffly. Brandi was tall and beautiful, and she knew it. She had long black hair and a body she proudly flaunted every chance she got. I always felt inferior next to her. She was three years older than I was, and I knew she and Chase dated in the past. She had dreams of becoming a model or an actress and always said she was just biding her time in this hick town until she hit it big. So far, she had only been an extra in the two movies that filmed in our town and was in a television commercial for the car dealership on the highway.

Most of Chase's girlfriends didn't understand our friendship and thought I was competition. Nothing could be further from the truth. Being an only child, Chase saw me as the kid sister he never had. We had that in common along with losing our mothers. We understood each other.

Before I could answer, Chase broke in, "Brandi, let Scott know I'm here and I want to talk to him. I'll meet him in his office in a minute. I want a slice of pecan pie with a scoop of chocolate ice cream, and Karsyn wants a slice of the buttermilk pie. Bring two coffees and make sure you bring lots of cream for Karsyn."

He pulled me into a hug as I laughed at his order. "Yeah, I know what you like. Personal Superman, remember? It's my job to know these things." He slid back out of the booth as Brandi walked away. "I'll be back in a few minutes." He walked down the short hall across from us and entered Scott's office, leaving the door open behind him.

I saw Scott hurry from the kitchen, wiping his hands on the apron he wore. As he approached his office, he paused and forced a tight smile before walking in and closing the door. I decided to wash up while he was gone. Brandi brought out our coffees and ignored me as I left.

I turned off the water after washing up and left the ladies' room. I heard Chase's voice as the office door opened, and he walked out.

"I want it done by tomorrow morning, Scott. I'll be very disappointed if it isn't," he stated, his voice cold and hard. As he turned, he saw me and smiled. I caught sight of Scott sitting in a chair across from his desk with his head in his hands before Chase closed the door behind him.

"What are you doing back here, Karsyn?" he asked, glancing back at the closed office door as he led me back to our booth.

"I had to wash my hands. My personal Superman was a little late with the rescue, and my hands were dirty," I explained, laughing as I held out my now clean hands.

He stared at me a moment, as if he were searching for something in my expression. I laughed at his seriousness and elbowed him in the side playfully. "Why so serious?" I accused.

His expression cleared, and he gestured for me to slide into the booth before him. "Sorry. Some things in business aren't very pleasant. Don't worry about it."

෪ ෭

Chase and I talked over our pie and coffee while I caught him up on the latest town gossip. I always thought it was funny how much he loved to hear about the rumors floating around Lucky Strike that had all the locals talking. He always said it was because he lived out on his family's large ranch, so he missed what was going on in town. He said I was a fountain of information and better than any newspaper he could pick up. Ha! I often reminded him that his family owned the Striker's Gazette so that wasn't my fault.

He walked me back to my car and held the door open as I got in. He shut the door and leaned down, propping his arms on my open window.

"So how's my cat doing?" he asked.

"My cat is fine." I grinned. He liked to claim part ownership of my cat and was only letting me keep her for him. "Sprite is fat and happy like always."

He double tapped the window opening with his knuckles before taking a step back from the car.

"I thought I'd come by and make sure you're taking good care of my cat. Maybe say hi to your dad," he said. "I have some details of our new contract I need to discuss with him."

I shrugged in reply. "That's fine. I know he's home. He's been having trouble with his back since he fell off that ladder a few weeks back. His back was giving him trouble again this morning, so he was going to take it easy."

Chase followed me as I drove to the edge of town and turned into the parking lot of my father's garage. Our cottage-style house was next door, so I walked across the yard to meet Chase at the door after he got out of his truck. Holding the screen door open for me so I could open the front door, he followed me inside.

"Dad?" I called out. I dropped my purse and keys on the hall table before kicking off my heels.

My height dropped three inches, causing Chase to chuckle. He pulled me into a playful hug and put his hand on the top of my head, reminding me again, I only came up to his chest instead of his chin when I wore my heels.

"Such a tiny little thing you are. Now you're perfect and my chin is safe from further damage," he teased.

"Ha. Ha." I smirked, punching him in the chest and sticking out my tongue.

"In here, Kari," my dad called. Gran had nicknamed me Kari when I was little, saying it was too confusing having two Carson's in the house and she couldn't very well call me Junior. She and Daddy were the only ones I allowed to call me Kari. I was proud to be my daddy's daughter, so never let anyone else call me by anything other than Karsyn.

He came from the kitchen, walking stiffly to the hall where we stood. He cut his gaze from me to Chase; his eyes narrowed slightly. "Oh, hello, Chase. I didn't expect to see you today."

"Just making sure Karsyn got home okay," he said as he released me to shake my father's hand.

My dad gestured for us to precede him into our small living room before sitting in his recliner.

"What happened, Kari?" my dad asked while looking at Chase for answers.

"I got a flat downtown. The car is next door so you can fix it tomorrow," I replied. "If you're not up to it, I can use your truck to go job hunting in the city." I purposely left out the part about changing the tire.

"I changed the tire for her. The tire's in her trunk. It had a nail in it, probably from driving by the construction site," Chase offered.

My dad looked at me a moment before sighing. "You couldn't change your tire, could you, Kari?"

My head dropped in embarrassment at the quiet accusation. "No, I had a little trouble with it," I mumbled. My eyes cut Chase an accusing glare for tattling, to which he just shrugged his shoulders.

"Traitor," I mumbled under my breath.

"It was no trouble, Carson. I'm just glad I was there to help. I like looking out for Karsyn," he assured my dad. "I want to discuss this year's contract with you, if you have time. There are a couple of details I want to go over with you before we renew."

My dad stood and cleared his throat. "Why don't we go next door to my office? I left the contract on my desk."

He walked up to me and hugged me, kissing my forehead. "Why don't you get dinner started while I visit with Chase? This shouldn't take too long."

I eyed them both curiously, but figured the tension suddenly coming from my father must be due to the pain he was in from getting up and down. Chase walked past us, heading for the door. "I'll meet you in your office," he said. "Take care, Karsyn. I'll see you later before I leave."

I looked back at my dad as I heard him sigh. The screen door slammed as Chase left the house. I heard his boots cross the porch and descend the steps. "Are you okay, Dad? I'm sure if you're hurting, Chase won't mind waiting until tomorrow or the next day to talk business," I suggested, rubbing his arm in comfort.

He shook his head at me and sighed again, staring out the window at the shop. "No, it's fine. I had a feeling this day was coming. I just need to get it over with. You stay here and start supper, okay? I'll be back soon." He hugged me again before slowly walking out.

CR ℘

I stepped out onto the porch and sat on the steps to wait for my dad to come back. After changing into denim shorts and a yellow halter-top, I opted to go barefoot. I had Sprite in my lap and absent-mindedly scratched her behind the ears. Dinner was simmering on the stove and would be ready soon. I turned as I heard my dad's voice coming from the open window in his office. My dad was always such a gentle man, so I was surprised at the anger in his voice.

"Damn it, Chase! I won't allow it!"

I couldn't make out Chase's reply but stood when I heard the door slam. I started down the porch steps as I saw Chase and my father coming out of the garage. My father looked grim and defeated. I hurried over to him.

"Daddy? Are you okay?" I glared at Chase standing beside him. "What did you do? I told you he wasn't well."

My dad pulled me into his arms and patted my back. "Now, don't you fuss, I'm fine. Chase didn't do anything to me. It's just business and sometimes negotiations get a little unpleasant," he assured me.

I huffed but hugged him in return.

"Well, I'm heading out. I'll have Doug call you Thursday to discuss the schedule for bringing in the trucks for their tune ups," Chase said.

Dad cleared his throat and stepped in front of me to shake Chase's proffered hand. "Yeah, you do that," he grumbled.

I stared, searching my father's face. With his voice laced with disapproval, he no longer seemed as friendly with Chase as he had always been in the past.

"Good luck with the job hunting, Karsyn. I hope you find something that doesn't take you away from our fair town. Your dad needs you, and I'd miss seeing you around," Chase said.

He smiled pleasantly at my dad, flashing his bright teeth. "Carson, I'm glad we could come to an understanding. It's always a pleasure doing business with you. Big name shops just don't have that personal touch your garage does. I don't know what this town would do without you. You take care of your back."

When I saw my dad stiffen, I looked questioningly between the two men in front of me. Chase smiled down at me and winked before walking to his truck. He waved as he pulled out of our driveway and drove down the street. I turned back to see my father glaring at the back of Chase's truck as it disappeared around the corner. His vision was filled with a hate I had never seen before. He glanced at me and cleared his expression, a fake smile plastered on his face.

"So what's for dinner?" he asked.

"Tacos," I answered blandly. I raised my eyebrow, showing my displeasure at being left in the dark. "Want to explain what that was all about?"

He sighed and started for the house, leaving me standing in the yard. "Maybe later. Right now, I need to think about some things." The firm set of his jaw told me there would be no discussion about what had just taken   place.

Chapter Three

July 2007

I smiled as the door to the restaurant opened. "Hi, Daddy," I said with a laugh. "You eat here more now that I'm working here than you ever did before."

I started working at the Double S the day after I was there with Chase. Brandi had been accused of stealing from the register and left town the same day she was fired. I was shocked when I found out. She always looked down her nose at me, the poor daughter of a mechanic, but I never thought of her as dishonest.

I was thrilled when Scott called and offered me Brandi's job. He said he heard I was job hunting. The pay was more than I thought it would be and the tips were amazing. I wouldn't need to look for a job anymore. In just six weeks, I'd already made enough money to take over my car payment and insurance from my dad and put a little money aside.

"Can't a father miss his little girl?" Dad chuckled and pulled me into a brief hug before releasing me.

"I love you too, Daddy. So, you want a table or booth today?" I asked.

"Booth, please. Gabe and I need to talk shop." My dad gestured to the man standing behind him that I had failed to notice. "I just hired him to help work at the shop. Thought I'd treat him to lunch before putting him to work."

A visit to the doctor showed that my dad needed back surgery, so he had to find help to keep the garage running. He mentioned he might hire someone; I just didn't realize he had already found someone. Lately, Dad seemed to keep a lot to himself, which concerned me. We always talked about everything. I worried things were worse with his back than he let on due to all the trips to the city to visit the doctor. He scheduled his appointments during my shift at the restaurant. All he would tell me was it was pre-op stuff before his surgery next month.

I turned my attention to the stranger with my dad and clenched my teeth to keep my jaw from dropping. Oh, my God! He was gorgeous. He had wavy black hair and eyes so dark they appeared almost black. When he smiled, the flash of teeth looked brilliant against his tan. His black t-shirt stretched across his chest, leaving no doubt to the definition lying underneath. The bands on the sleeves strained against his muscular arms. God, I wished he would turn around so I could see his ass in those jeans. It was certain to be just as gorgeous as the rest of him. I suppressed the little shudder that went through me at the thought.

"Gabe, this is Karsyn, my little girl. Kari, this is Gabriel Thompson, my new mechanic."

"Gabe, please. Only my mother calls me Gabriel," he replied, flashing his smile at me again.

He reached out to shake my hand, and I smiled in return. "Don't like being named after an angel, or are you just not one?" I smirked.

I had no idea where that had come from. I wasn't a flirt, especially in front of my dad or with strangers. Too many broken hearts in my past had made me wary, and I rarely put forth the effort. I would flirt, a guy would be interested, we'd go out a couple of times, and he'd dump me like a hot brick for no apparent reason.

"Little of both, I guess," he said, laughing.

"Kari, that's enough. I need Gabe here to focus on the job he came to do," Dad chided. His eyes narrowed at Gabe.

"Not a problem, Carson. I'm too old for her anyway," Gabe assured my dad.

"Too old? What are you thirty or something?" I snarked, looking him up and down. I don't know why, but I wanted him to be interested in me. There was just something about him. It was irritating that he could dismiss me so easily.

"Not for three more years. And you're what, seventeen?" he shot back with a smirk, looking me up and down in return.

"I'll have you know, I turned eighteen back in April, smartass."

I put my hands on my hips in a huff. I couldn't believe I was arguing and flirting on the job and in front of my dad. I grabbed a couple of menus, walked over to a nearby booth, and dropped them on the table. When I heard my father clear his voice, I suspected Gabe was staring at my backside clad in my short skirt.

I turned around to face him. I held my breath as his gaze slowly traveled from my head to my toes, causing my body to respond immediately, before finally meeting my eyes again. He quirked his lip, clearly not embarrassed I'd caught him staring. I sniffed distastefully and turned to my dad to see his worried expression darting between us. I grinned and hugged my dad. He was always a worrywart when it came to me.

"I love you, Daddy, and I'm glad you got help for the shop. You sit down and I'll go get your coffee.

He patted my back and slid into the booth. "You're a good girl, Kari. You take really good care of your old man. I couldn't ask for better than you." I turned to walk away but stopped when a warm hand grasped mine.

"I'll take coffee, too, in case you're interested."

I looked down at the hand holding mine before raising my eyes to lock gazes with the man before me. "I'm not, but I'll get your coffee anyway," I said condescendingly.

My back stiffened at the deep chuckle coming from him as I left. "That's quite a spitfire of a daughter you have there, Carson."

"Just remember why you're here and leave my daughter alone."

ᎣᎡ ᎦᎠ

I stood at the counter wrapping silverware and sneaking peeks at my father's booth while he and Gabe talked shop. I caught bits and pieces of their conversation when I wasn't serving other customers. It was always something mechanical, which I didn't understand or care about. I huffed and glared at the back of Gabe's head again before dropping another container of silverware on the counter, causing it to rattle loudly. Dad glanced up briefly at me over Gabe's shoulder, his expression filled with concern. I smiled reassuringly at him and shrugged before focusing again on my task. Just then, the door opened, and I grinned. At least here was someone who would listen to me rant about being ignored.

"Heather!" I squealed. "Oh, my God! When did you get back in town?" I ran from behind the counter and grabbed my best friend in a hug.

"Karsyn! Mom said you were working here. I just got in today. I dropped my suitcase at the house, said hi to Mom, and came straight here."

A throat cleared behind me, and I turned to find Gabe smiling arrogantly as his gaze shifted between Heather and me. I could almost hear the thought in his mind. "See? too immature." I fought the urge to stick out my tongue at him and prove his point. Instead, I turned my back on him in a huff. My spine stiffened at the deep chuckle coming from him.

"Hey, Papa C." Heather walked over to their booth and leaned down to give my dad a hug. She straightened back up and turned to Gabe. "And just who is this fine hunk of man sitting here looking all lonely? You're new in town."

She let her gaze wander over his chest and shifted so she was leaning against the side of the booth, smoothing her hand down her shirt to draw attention to herself. Heather had long straight blonde hair and blue eyes. Taller than me by a couple of inches, she looked like a runway model. My dad laughed, and I rolled my eyes at her. Heather was a world-class flirt and could give lessons in how it was done. She liked to flirt shamelessly but was completely harmless. She enjoyed the chase but rarely kept a boyfriend more than couple of weeks. No one measured up to her exacting standards enough to keep around. She was looking for Mr. Right, and anyone else was not worth wasting her time.

We had been best friends since kindergarten. Her family lived two streets over from us. We spent so much time at each other's homes that we actually kept clothes and toothbrushes to save the trouble of packing every couple of days for sleepovers. She was the sister I never had, and her mom and dad were as much like my second family as my dad was to her. Her dad worked in the city at an engineering firm, and her mom taught at the junior high school. Heather left right after graduation to stay with her grandparents in Sweden. I usually went with her but couldn't this year due to dad's bad back.

I laughed at Gabe's expression of fear. Yeah, Heather could do that to you if you didn't know better. My dad laughed also and patted Heather's arm.

"Heather, you're going to scare my new mechanic off, and I need him. Gabe, this is Heather, Kari's best friend and daughter of my heart."

Daughter of my heart was how Dad always referred to Heather. It always earned him a kiss on the cheek, which Heather was quick to plant now.

"Aw, Papa C, I love you, too. Mom gave me a pan of pecan brownies for you; they're in the car. I was going to drop them by the shop after visiting with Karsyn."

"Tell your mom thanks. She knows how much I love those brownies." Dad smiled.

"Come on, Karsyn. Let's go catch up. I have to tell you about my trip. I met the cutest guy." She laughed and pulled me back to the counter so we could gossip about her love life in relative privacy.

Just as she began describing her latest conquest, the door opened again, admitting Chase and his ranch foreman. I excused myself from Heather and went to greet them.

"Hi, Chase. Hi, Mr. Kent." I grabbed a couple of menus and started walking them back to the corner booth where Chase always sat.

"Karsyn, look at you all grown up now," Mr. Kent greeted me as he slid into the booth. "Chase, when are you going to snatch up this pretty girl? If you don't, I might just be tempted to pull out the old charm and dust it off." When he smiled, his eyes twinkled.

"Mr. Kent, you old flirt. You don't fool me. I know all about your Saturday dinners with Harriet Weimer. I ran into her at the store this morning, buying a roast for your dinner tonight." I shook my finger at him playfully.

He laughed in return, taking the menu from me.

"Who's the man with your dad?" Chase asked, still standing, staring across the restaurant at my dad's booth.

I put his menu in front of him and shrugged. "He's the new mechanic my dad hired. His name is Gabe. Would you like two coffees to start?" I asked, wanting to change the subject.

"Sure, and two lunch specials, also. I think I'll go say hello to your dad." Chase headed back to the front and stopped at my dad's booth.

I turned in their order and went back to visit with Heather, keeping one ear on the snippets of conversation coming from the booth across from me.

"If you needed help, you should have asked. Bobby mentioned the other day about looking for extra work on the side," Chase said.

"Bobby works for you, Chase. I can hire my own employees. Thanks anyway," Dad replied stiffly. It was easy to see by the tension in his shoulders that he was angry about something.

"Well, no need to hire some stranger you don't know. There are plenty of able-bodied men in town who'd be happy to help you out. I can make a few calls if you like. You have Karsyn to think about. How do you know this guy here won't hurt her or, at the least, rob you blind?"

Dad stood and pulled out his wallet to throw some money on the table. Gabe stood with him, eyeing Chase thoughtfully. My dad turned slowly to face Chase and stared at him a moment.

"Gabe isn't a stranger. His dad and I were in the service together. If there's one man I trust with my business or my daughter more than myself, it's him. You let me worry about my daughter's safety and my business. I may have to do business with you, but I don't have to like you." My dad's eyes cut from Heather to me as we watched their exchange.

He smiled tightly at me. "Kari, I'll see you at home after your shift. You be careful and come straight home. Heather, come over tomorrow for dinner and tell your mom thanks again for the brownies."

I watched in shock as my father and Gabe left and climbed into his truck. I had never seen him treat Chase that way. He was always friendly and polite. I turned to Chase, who was staring out the window at the parking lot with narrowed eyes. He turned and winked at me as though nothing was wrong.

"I guess the painkillers are affecting your dad's personality. I hear they can do that," he offered as an excuse as he walked passed me to his booth. "I hope he doesn't get worse. Painkillers are dangerous and can really mess a person up."

Chapter Four

December 1, 2007

Heather helped me put my hair up, securing the French twist with rhinestone pins while I applied lip gloss. After spending the last two hours getting ready, I stared critically at my reflection in the mirror. I sucked in my cheeks and then released them. A few curls framed my face softening the look. I was wearing a short, velvet, hunter-green, a-line dress and black high heels.

"Ugh, I need to go on a diet. Working at the restaurant is making me fat," I groaned, pressing my hand against my stomach and sucking in.

"You look fantastic, Karsyn. Gabe isn't going to know what hit him." Heather grinned wickedly and wiggled her eyebrows suggestively at me in the bathroom mirror.

"I want everyone in town to see us tonight. I'm tired of hiding," I snapped.

"It was your idea to keep your relationship a secret all this time," she teased with a giggle.

"Don't remind me. I only did it to protect Daddy. I didn't want to upset him during his recovery."

I took a deep breath to calm the butterflies in my stomach. I didn't know why I was so nervous. Gabe and I had been seeing each other since August, but tonight would be the first time we would go out openly as a couple. Gabe was taking me to the Christmas parade and dance. Heather and Dad were the only people who knew we had been dating for the past four months.

I was afraid how my dad would handle our relationship, so I insisted we keep things quiet until after he fully recovered from his operation. Dad had his back surgery at the end of July and suffered a heart attack during the procedure. I didn't want anything to upset his recovery. Heather knew from the beginning. I used her as my smoke screen to slip away to visit Gabe at his rented house across town or to meet in the city. I hated sneaking around, but all of our stolen moments did add an air of excitement to our relationship.

Everything worked out fine until last week when Dad walked in on us kissing in his office in the shop. He actually took the news better than I thought he would. He and Gabe had a long private talk before giving us his blessing. He wasn't thrilled with our age difference, but he only wanted my happiness.

I flirted shamelessly with Gabe in the beginning. If I hadn't been certain he was the one for me, I would have been ashamed of myself. He fought me every step of the way that first month. He had tried to ignore me when I'd wander into the garage in my halter-tops and short denim skirts while he was bent over an engine or was trapped under a car. Sometimes I would sunbathe in the yard in my tiny black bikini while he took his break or ate lunch on the patio behind the shop. I knew I affected him by how hard he fought; there was a hunger in his eyes when he thought I wasn't looking. I was diligent, making sure he stayed hydrated during the hot summer months, bringing him cold drinks from the house even though they had a refrigerator and vending machine at the shop.

Nothing seemed to work, and I was discouraged. I was ready to admit defeat when things changed the Sunday before Dad's surgery.

"I swear each and every time I pull this damn thing out, I won't put it back here again," I mumbled to myself.

I stood on my tiptoes, straining to reach the platter I only used for holidays. Every year I questioned why I kept it stored on the top shelf of the cabinet. I was making a last ditch effort to gain Gabe's attention. If I couldn't do it with flirting, then maybe it was time to go back to basics.

Dad invited Gabe to dinner, and my grandmother always said, "The fastest way to a man's heart was through his stomach." So there I was, killing myself by cooking a huge feast in the middle of summer and using our fancy serving dishes instead of just putting the pots on the table like I normally would. Dad shot me a few looks when he saw me setting the table with our good china. I used the excuse that I wanted to make dinner special since he was going in for surgery tomorrow.

Yeah, that sounded weak to me too, but desperate times called for desperate measures. I mean, I had a turkey roasting in the oven, cornbread and bread stuffing since I wasn't sure what Gabe would like, my grandmother's sweet rice, squash, broccoli and cheese sauce, and a huge salad. I even made homemade yeast rolls and an Italian Crème Cake from scratch for dessert.

I strained a little further and managed to hook my finger on the edge of the platter. "Gotcha!" I exclaimed proudly. I grabbed hold of the dish and stepped back on the chair only to find nothing but air under my foot. "Shit!"

I screamed as I fell and closed my eyes against the pain I knew I was coming. I heard my platter break on the floor as I felt strong arms grab me around the waist, and I fell against a hard chest. "I've got you," a deep voice said reassuringly.

I tilted my head to see my savior and flushed in embarrassment when I realized Gabe was the one who caught me. I started to thank him for saving me but the sound died on my tongue as I stared, mesmerized by the emotions flickering in his eyes. He turned me so I was facing him, his hands tightening on my hips before pulling me so we were flush against each other.

"This is such a bad idea," he mumbled. Lust flared in his eyes as my hands slid across his chest, feeling the muscles under his shirt. My tongue darted out to wet my lips, and his eyes watched the motion. "Fuck it. I'm going to hell for this."

His lips crashed against mine, and his tongue demanded entrance into my mouth. I gladly parted my lips to his assault and drank in the feeling of his tongue exploring my mouth. My tongue stroked his and battled for the opportunity to plunge into his mouth, tasting him. The growl resonated deep in his chest as my fingers curled into his hair, tugging slightly. I was so afraid if he stopped kissing me, he would come to his senses and remember he thought I was too young for him.

"Please don't stop," I whimpered when he finally pulled away. We needed to breathe, but I didn't want to.

"I couldn't stop if someone paid me," he said softly. His hand reached to brush my hair back from my face before he lowered his head again. This time the kiss was soft and gentle against my swollen lips. I moaned into his mouth as his arms tightened around me again. We finally broke apart when I heard the front door slam and my father calling for us.

I smiled as I remembered the weeks that followed. He kept me company while I waited for the outcome of Dad's surgery. He held me as I cried when the surgeon gave me the news of his heart attack and all through the first night Dad was in ICU. That first week, he drove me to the hospital each morning and brought me home each evening. He stayed with me at night until Dad came home so he didn't worry I wasn't sleeping. He was wonderful to me, and every day I fell more in love with him.

Tonight we were going on a double date with Heather and her newest beau, Andrew. Tonight everyone would know Gabe was my boyfriend. No more watching women flirt with him while I stood by pretending it didn't piss me off. More than once, I'd wanted to crawl onto his lap at the restaurant and eat him alive just to keep women from brushing their bodies against his. He laughed at me the day I suggested he parade down Main Street without a shirt to show off the claw marks on his back and the hickey on his chest proving he was unavailable.

I huffed and turned this way and that in front of the mirror. "Brandi Miller, eat your heart out," I mumbled.

"Karsyn, why even bring her up? I know she gave you a hard time in the past, but no one has even heard from her since she moved away. Let it go already." Heather rolled her eyes in reply.

"You're right. It's just hard to let go of old grudges sometimes. She always made me feel small," I sighed.

"Karsyn, I hate to break it to you, but you are small. Tiny." Heather held her hand up showing a miniscule space between her thumb and forefinger. She laughed and hugged me before walking away to grab her purse. "I've got to run. Andrew is picking me up from my house soon. We'll meet you at Double S in a few."

᎒Ꮞ ᎒Ꮞ

Gabe's black truck pulled into the drive, and I ogled him from my bedroom window. Even from a distance, he looked so good in his black jacket; starched, white, button-down shirt; pressed jeans; and boots. I listened for Dad to let him in the house and checked my appearance once more before heading downstairs.

I smiled as his voice drifted up the stairs.

"I'm still not sure about this. I'm worried," Dad was saying.

"This may be just the thing we need. So far, all we've got are rumors and speculation. Nothing concrete enough to nail down. He's too careful and no one will talk. You know how things work here better than I do." He paused before sighing. "She's the only weakness I've found the entire time I've been here. He won't sit idly by for this," Gabe replied. "Trust me. He'll make a move and we'll be ready."

"You just watch out for my little girl. You keep her safe. Promise," Dad demanded.

"This isn't a game for me, Carson. It may be too soon, but I love her. I want you to know that when this is over, I plan on coming clean and asking her to marry me," Gabe replied. "She needs to be told. I don't like keeping her in the dark. It's too dangerous."

I stood stunned by his words. My hands flew to my mouth to stifle my squeal. None of their conversation made any sense to me, but I didn't care. All that mattered was Gabe loved me! He wanted to marry me! I fought the urge to jump up and down, and rush into the room screaming, "Yes, I'll marry you!"

I took a deep breath to calm my nerves. I turned and tiptoed back up several steps before turning and coming back down, stepping a little harder so they would hear me.

CR 80

We talked and laughed with Heather and Andrew through dinner. Afterward, Gabe and I walked down the street to the square. I stood watching the Christmas parade wrapped in Gabe's arms, surrounded by his warmth as I sipped hot chocolate. I couldn't wait for the night to end. I wanted to go back to his house, lie in his arms, and tell him how much I loved him too. I leaned my head against his chest and sighed.

"Are you cold?" he asked, as he shrugged off his jacket and wrapped it around me.

"No, just happy," I replied softly. I tilted my face up as his came down to brush my lips with a kiss.

"I'm glad, Karsyn. I want you to be happy," he whispered. He straightened and scanned the thinning crowd. Everyone was leaving to go home or to the dance. He looked down at me again and pulled me close. "You ready to go dancing?"

He led me back to his truck and opened the passenger door for me. A voice called my name from the distance as I began to climb in the cab. I stopped and turned to see Chase crossing the street. He was dressed similar to Gabe in a jacket and dark jeans.

"Hello, Karsyn. Don't you look sweet tonight?" Chase grinned, pulling me to him and swinging me up into one of his hugs. "So sweet, I may need to take a nibble." He leaned in and nipped playfully at my neck before setting me down again. He kept me tucked into his side with his arm around my shoulders.

I slapped his chest and laughed. "Chase Carter, don't you ever get tired of using the same old lines? I don't know what all the girls see in you. I think you've been using that same tired line for as long as I've known you." I turned to Gabe and smiled, reaching out my hand to clasp his. "You remember Gabe, don't you?"

Gabe took the opportunity to pull me from Chase's side and lifted me up to sit in his truck; he then stepped in front of me, blocking me from Chase's view. I smiled at the possessive behavior. Annoyance flashed in Chase's eyes at the gesture.

"I remember the mechanic," he sneered. "By the way, that truck you worked on the other day isn't running right. It has a rattle in the engine that wasn't there before. I plan on discussing your incompetence with your employer soon.

31

"I told Bobby when he picked the truck up that it needed a new clutch. It's not my problem if he didn't relay the message. I made note of it in the maintenance log, and he signed it," Gabe replied calmly. "I assure you, Carson is aware of it as well. He plans to call you this week to schedule when you want to bring it back in."

"Well, I guess it's a good thing you're so diligent. Tell Carson I look forward to his call," Chase replied before turning to me again.

"You don't need to leave, Karsyn. It's nice of you to take pity on him and take him to the parade, but you look too pretty to go home so early. I was coming over to invite you to go dancing with me." Chase smiled and winked.

He stepped forward to reach for me, but Gabe blocked him by closing my door. I heard the locks engage and since the windows were up, I was shut out of the conversation taking place just a few feet from me.

I did manage to hear Gabe tell Chase that I already had a date to the dance before walking around to the driver's side of the truck. He unlocked the door and climbed in, started the engine and backed out, leaving Chase standing on the street. I shrugged as an offer of apology and waved to him as we drove off before turning to Gabe. I stared at him, waiting for him to explain his behavior. It soon became apparent that he wasn't going to make any attempt to explain.

"That was extremely rude. What's your problem with Chase, anyway?" I demanded.

Gabe pulled into the gravel parking lot for the VFW Hall and parked. He shut off the engine and sat staring into the darkness. After a moment, he got out and slammed his door, causing me to jump. I watched him warily as he came around and opened my door. He unbuckled my seatbelt and pulled my legs around so he stood between my knees. He grasped my face between his hands, and I stared into his eyes, not understanding the torture swimming in their depths. I smoothed his furrowed brow with my fingertips.

"Talk to me, Gabe. Why are you so upset? Is it Chase? Don't worry, I'll talk to Daddy. You won't lose your job," I reassured him.

He chuckled and leaned back to stare at me. "I'm not worried about my job, Karsyn. Your dad's not going to fire me over anything Chase Carter says to him. I want you to stay away from Chase, though. Can you do that for me?" he asked.

I searched his face for answers that weren't forthcoming. My brow wrinkled in confusion at his demand. "Why would I stay away from Chase? We've been friends for years. He's one of my best friends. You don't need to be jealous or anything. Chase only sees me as his little sister," I shrugged.

He sighed heavily and leaned in to kiss me. His fingers speared my hair undoing my twist and releasing the pins. Several pins fell on the leather seat and floor, forgotten in our moment of passion. When we both finally came up for air, he combed out my locks with his fingers, removing the last of the pins still dangling in my hair.

"Sometimes I forget how young and naïve you are, Karsyn. There are things going on you don't understand. Promise me you'll stay away from him," he stressed.

I shook my head at him and slid off the seat to stand and face him. "I'm sorry but I can't promise that. There's no reason for you to try and warn me away from him. Whatever is going on between you two, you need to get over. Chase has always been a good friend to me. Unless you can give me a reason, then he's going to continue to be my friend." I wrapped my arms around his neck pulling his lips down to mine and kissed him again. When he pulled away, I stroked his cheek with my fingers. "Please, let's not fight tonight, Gabe. I want to go inside and dance. Then later I want to go back to your place and have you make love to me."

I didn't understand the struggle in his eyes. He seemed to lose whatever internal battle he was waging with himself and sighed, defeated. He shut the truck door and pulled me closer, and I felt the tension in his arms. "I just want you safe, Karsyn. I don't know what I'd do if I lost you," he said softly.

I smiled up at him and hugged him tighter. "Don't worry. You'll never lose me."

Chapter Five

I stood at the edge of the dance floor, visiting with a couple of friends from high school while Gabe went to get me a soda. I secretly felt a little smug with their reactions to finding out Gabe was with me. I'd been the odd man out for so long. The hair on my neck was damp, making me hot and chilled at the same time. I fanned my face with my hand in an attempt to dry the perspiration on my throat. Gabe and I had danced almost every song since we came in. I loved to dance, and he was happy to oblige.

I jumped when arms encircled my waist from behind, pulling me against a hard chest. The cologne smelled wrong. I turned my head to see who was holding me and my eyes opened wide in surprise. His eyes danced with amusement as he spun me around and lifted my feet off the ground, carrying me to the dance floor before setting me down again. Holding me close, he immediately began moving us across the floor to the slow beat of the country song played by the band.

"Chase Carter, shame on you! You scared the shit out of me!" I laughed.

"Sorry for scaring you, but I've been waiting to dance with you all night. I was just about to have that damn mechanic thrown out if he didn't leave you alone for five minutes so I could get my dance," he scowled, his eyes narrowing. "And don't cuss. You're a lady."

I shook my head and laughed at him. "Yes, Daddy. But you can't do that. He's my date. How would I ever get home?"

He pushed me away, holding my hand to turn me in a spin before bringing me back flush against his chest. I grabbed his shoulder to keep from stumbling at the unexpected move. It was a slow song; one that didn't call for spinning. We were so close now that with every step, his leg slid in between mine and his arm tightened around my waist, preventing me from moving back to a comfortable distance. I tried to search for Gabe, but couldn't find him through the crush of people on the dance floor. The longer we danced, the more uncomfortable I became. Chase never held me like this before. I wondered if he was drunk and just didn't realize how tight his hold was.

"Have you been drinking?" I leaned in to sniff but couldn't smell any alcohol on him.

"No, I haven't been drinking. And how do you think you'd get home? The same way you always do. Me," he stated, as if it was the most obvious answer.

I always ended up at these dances without a date and usually had to beg Heather and her date for a ride home. Chase would invariably come to my rescue, spend the evening dancing with me, and make sure I got home so Heather was free to go parking with her date at the end of the night.

I patted his shoulder. "Well tonight you're off the hook. I have a date, and he's going to take me home. You can hook up with whoever the flavor of the month is and make her dreams come true."

The flash anger in his eyes surprised me. He seemed to think about his next response, took my hand, and brought it up to place on his other shoulder before using his hand to cup the back of my head and lacing his fingers in my hair. He tilted my head back so I was staring into his eyes. He ran his fingers through my hair, bringing it forward to drape over my shoulder. The gesture was too intimate and my stomach tightened nervously.

"What if I like giving you a ride home?" he whispered. His eyes sparkled with some softer emotion then hardened with a look of determination before he spoke again. "I think it's time you and I-"

"Mind if I cut in?"

With a firm hand, Gabe grasped my elbow and quickly pulled me out of Chase's arms before spinning me into his. The suddenness of the move prevented Chase from stopping him, taking him and me by surprise. I sighed in relief at the feeling of security that came over me from being back in Gabe's arms.

"Yes, I do mind," Chase sneered.

He reached to pull me back, causing Gabe to tighten his hold around me and angle his body between us.

"Hey-" I started, trying to diffuse the situation, only to be interrupted by Gabe. Things were quickly getting out of hand between the two of them. Even though I was uncomfortable during my dance with Chase, people were beginning to stare, embarrassing me.

"Well that's too damn bad, because she's my date, and I'm a firm believer in dancing with the one that brought you. So if you'll excuse us, we were just leaving."

Gabe ushered me from the dance floor, preventing Chase from responding or doing anything other than staring after us as we left the hall. I clenched my teeth, seething in anger and embarrassment at his actions. I didn't want to cause a scene in front of everyone, though, so I let him lead me out into the cold night. Once we cleared the entrance and were halfway through the dark parking lot, however, I stopped and jerked away from him.

"What the hell?" I snapped. "That's twice tonight you've been rude to Chase. All we did is dance. You have no right to act the way you did!" I ignored my twinge of conscience, remembering that I didn't like the way Chase had danced with me.

He watched me dispassionately while I yelled at him, only making me angrier. I screamed in frustration and stomped my foot at him.

"Are you finished? Got it all out of your system now?" he asked calmly.

"I'm warning you Gabe, don't do that," I seethed. "Do not treat me like a child."

"I won't treat you like a child when you quit stomping your foot like one. You're my date, not his. You dance with me, not him." He pulled me into his arms and cupped my face with his hands, tilting my face up to his. His lips lowered until they brushed against my ear. "Stay away from him, Karsyn. You're mine," he growled lowly.

My eyes closed against my will, and I couldn't stop the shiver that ran down my spine at his words or prevent the whimper that escaped my lips as his mouth found that special place on my neck and sucked gently. All thoughts of anger washed away in an instant. I didn't even remember why I was mad at him. I just wanted more.

"Gabe," I whimpered.

"Who do you want, Karsyn?" He spoke the words softly against my lips.

"You, Gabe. Only you."

My fingers clenched in his shirt, and I stretched the fraction of an inch it took to seal the kiss. His lips crushed mine and stole my breath as he dominated my senses. No thought existed in my head other than Gabe. With butterflies building in my stomach and an ache deep inside me yearning for more, I released his shirt and buried my hands in his hair. I clutched handfuls of his locks and tried to draw him closer. I captured his tongue between my teeth, refusing to release him when he tried to pull away, sucking and stroking him with my own tongue. He pulled away as I ran out of breath and had to relinquish my hold.

"Not here, baby. Just hang on for a few minutes until I can get you home. I want to take my time with you," he promised.

I nodded my consent, unable to speak while I worked to catch my breath. He put his arm around me and ushered us to his truck.

○R   ℂ

I knelt on his bed and unbuttoned his shirt, kissing each new inch of skin displayed before me as he gathered my hair in his fists, groaning. I leaned down and kissed his navel as he pulled off his shirt and tossed it at the chair in the room. I have no idea if it made it or not. I began to work at unbuttoning his jeans.

"Not tonight, baby," he said softly. "I need something else from you."

I rose up again as he pulled me up and cupped my face in his hands. His thumbs rubbed at my cheeks, and I closed my eyes, sighing. I sensed him leaning in and tilted my face up to meet his. Tonight his kiss was different. There was a new gentleness in his touch, which made me remember the words I'd overheard him speak to my father.

I opened my eyes as he pulled away to find the familiar lust burning in his eyes, but now they held another emotion as well. I wrapped my arms around his waist and laid my head against his chest, listening to the steady sound of his heartbeat as he lowered the zipper of my dress. I raised my arms as he pulled the dress up over my head and threw it behind him. Tonight it would be different between us. It wouldn't just be sex. Tonight we would show our love for one another.

I couldn't stop the tiny shiver running down my spine at the hunger I saw in his eyes as he stared at me in my black bra and panties. His arms encircled my waist as he leaned in to plant a soft kiss between my breasts. His calloused hands slid slowly up my sides before reaching behind me to unclasp my bra. He tossed it to places unknown as he put his knee on the bed and guided me down into the soft comforter, pressing me into the mattress with his weight.

He held himself up by his elbows and stroked my hair away from my face for several moments, not speaking, just staring into my eyes. I knew he could see my love for him. My heart was so full, I felt like it could explode at any moment. I wondered if other people ever felt the intensity of love I felt for Gabe. I needed to tell him before it overwhelmed me. I opened my mouth to speak, and he placed a finger over my lips.

"Shhh."

He kissed me gently as my fingers ran over the contours of his shoulders and back. He began to place soft, open-mouthed kisses along my jaw, stopping to suck on my earlobe. I shivered in response and felt the goose bumps on my arms.

"Close your eyes, Karsyn. I want you to feel what you mean to me tonight," he whispered against my ear.

He continued the path down my neck, stopping again to suck and nip at the sensitive spot on my shoulder before flicking my nipple with his tongue. I sucked in a breath at the sensation and groaned as his lips encircled the hard nub, suckling deeply. Arching my back as my hands went to his head, I couldn't get close enough. I needed more. I heard the whimper escape my lips from his teeth grazing the tender flesh and the strain of fabric tearing at my hips. After a few moments of my needy whimpering, his lips continued their slow path down my abdomen, sucking at my waist and causing me to giggle.

"Good to know," he chuckled darkly, leaning in to suck at the same spot again. He held me as I squirmed, trying to break his hold on my flesh.

"Gabe, please stop, it tickles," I begged, completely out of breath.

I loved this about Gabe. He was always so intense and serious like the weight of the world rested on his shoulders. Yet all of that melted away when we were together in bed, leaving a very thorough but playful lover. I sucked in my breath and mewled loudly as his mouth closed over me. He had moved so swiftly, I wasn't even aware of it until his tongue stroked over me. His fingers slid inside me slowly while his tongue played with my bud. I writhed and moaned, my body building to an inferno that would engulf me if I didn't find release soon.

"Please Gabe, make love to me," I moaned. "I need you!"

I screamed as he nibbled my sensitive flesh, pressing his fingers against that place deep inside me. My back arched off the bed and my toes curled into the mattress as the inferno exploded and rushed through my body. My hands clawed at his shoulders; to push him away or pull him closer, I didn't know. I only knew I was feeling too much.

Gabe rose to his knees and pulled me up to straddle his waist. I wrapped my arms around him and buried my face in his neck as I slid down on him, still quaking in my orgasm. His groan mingled in the air with my whimper at the sensation of our joining, and I held him tighter. He grasped my hips, helping me adjust and set the pace. His lips conquered mine, and I submitted willingly to his domination. As our pace increased, he shifted us so I was lying on my back again with him over me, my legs locked around his waist.

My hands sought his hair and back alternately, trying to find a way to pull him ever closer. I wanted to crawl into his skin so we could become one. I arched against him, needing to feel him against every part of my flesh. The burning in the pit of my stomach grew as he brought me closer to a singular kind of explosion, knowing this time we would ignite together.

I could feel my orgasm so close. I felt a tear leak from the corner of my eye. My emotions were all over the place and the tension building inside of me was more than I could handle.

"Open your eyes, baby. Look at me. See me."

He held my face in his hands, and I stared, mesmerized by his eyes as he continued to thrust into me. In that moment, I saw a plethora of emotions churning inside him—lust, desire, need, and love. The same emotions reflected in his dark brown eyes as he stared back at me. The beginning of my orgasm took me as he leaned in and softly brushed his lips against mine.

"Oh, God, Gabe, I love you!" I screamed.

I shuddered and cried out as the sensations washed over me in a tidal wave of emotion. I lost sensation in my arms and legs; the force of my orgasm was so intense. I swear I even saw stars as my vision went black. I had never felt anything like this before. It was the single greatest feeling I'd ever experienced, and I knew it was because I loved him.

"I love you, Karsyn," he roared as his back arched and he shuddered, driving deep inside me repeatedly as he sought his own release. He fell on top of me and kissed me deeply. I gave him all my love in that kiss and felt it given to me in return. When he broke away, we were both panting heavily and slick with sweat. I closed my eyes and smiled as I sensed him shift to lie beside me and nestled my back into his chest, drifting into a contented sleep.

Chapter Six

Two weeks later

I slammed my car door shut and screamed at the top of my lungs, tightly gripping the steering wheel in anger. I heard Gabe calling me and quickly locked the doors and started the engine. He strode purposefully toward me from the shop where I'd left him after another argument. I shook my head at him as he yelled and gestured for me to get out of the car.

I backed out of the driveway, spinning gravel and almost hitting our mailman as he pulled up to the curb. As I drove off, I glared at my cell phone ringing in the passenger seat where I'd thrown it. I let it go to voicemail, but it immediately started ringing again. I took my eyes off the road a moment to grab my phone, flipping it open.

"What?" I snapped.

"Karsyn, get your ass back here right now! Are you fucking crazy? You almost hit the fucking postman! You don't even have a coat or your license on you! I swear to God, Karsyn, I will put you over my knee and give you the whipping your daddy should have given you years ago if you're not back here in five minutes! You do not leave in the middle of a discussion. That's immature and childish!"

I stared at the phone and stuck my tongue out at it, knowing Gabe couldn't see me prove his point at just how childish I could be before putting the phone back to my ear.

"Don't you threaten me, Gabriel Thompson. It's a small town. If I get pulled over, the sheriff knows who I am. I'm not some child you can push around. That wasn't a discussion. A discussion is where two people express their opinions and discuss them, coming to an agreement. You just demanded I do what you say. You wouldn't even listen to my side!" I sniffed, hating that when I got angry, my body's response was to start crying.

"Chase is my friend. Why can't you understand that? What can you possibly have against him?" I begged, trying not to breakdown. "Please. I love you, but you're making me choose between you and my best friend. I won't do that."

He growled in frustration before sighing. His voice dropped to a calm, persuasive tone. "Karsyn, please just come home, baby, and we'll talk about it. Okay?"

"No. Not right now," I said stubbornly. I refused to give in. I was right. He was wrong.

"Karsyn, turn around this instant and come home." I heard the warning tone in his voice.

"Please give me a little time. I promise I'll be home soon, and we can talk then. I just can't do it right now." I hated the way my voice cracked at the end.

He sighed again, this time in defeat. "I love you so much, baby. Please come home. I promise we'll talk, no yelling."

I smiled sadly. All I wanted to do was turn around and go home to him. I wanted him to hold me and make me feel secure in his love. If only he would get over this irrational jealousy of Chase. I sighed in defeat. I wasn't ready to talk, and I knew we'd just start arguing again the minute I pulled in the driveway. He was angry. I was angry. I couldn't handle another fight. I needed a break.

"I love you, too. Tell Daddy I'll be home soon. I promise." I snapped my phone shut and quickly turned it off before it could start ringing again. I loved him so much, but I was tired of fighting. I didn't even understand the reasons for our arguments. Before we went public, our relationship was wonderful, but ever since the night of the dance, it seemed all we did was fight. And every disagreement centered on my friendship with Chase.

I drove around town, not really knowing where I was going. Heather wasn't home today, and I didn't really want to talk to her about the fight, anyway. She didn't think any guy was worth being upset over, so her advice was to break up with Gabe or give in to what he wanted. She always took the easy path. Heather hated confrontations and avoided them at all costs.

When I ran a stop sign, almost causing another accident, I pulled off on the side of the road and parked. In one respect, Gabe was right; I was too upset to drive. I left the car, tossed my cell phone under the seat, and took only my keys with me. I didn't want to talk to anyone anyway. I stuffed my hands in the pockets of my jeans, trying to dismiss the cold air, which seeped in through my sweatshirt. I walked down the street, ignoring the few cars that passed by.

I ended up at the park and walked over to the playground. I sat on the swings, and as I stared at the pond in front of me, I finally gave in to my emotions and started crying. I looked up at the sound of a truck door slamming before dropping my chin to my chest, sighing. I didn't want to see anyone right now. Wiping my tears on my sleeve, I raised my head again and stared at the water as he walked over to me.

I gave him a weak smile when I felt his presence and his eyes on me for a moment before he stepped behind me. I felt the pull on the swing, setting it in motion and smiled again. He pushed me in silence, seeming to know what I needed.

"You've been crying," he said after a while.

I didn't respond.

"Want to talk about it?"

"No," I said quietly.

He continued to push me in silence.

"Why are men so stupid?" I finally asked, turning to look at him over my shoulder. "He won't listen to me, and I don't understand."

"Your dad?"

I shook my head at him and sighed. "No."

His brow wrinkled in confusion. "Is this about the mechanic?"

"His name is Gabe, Chase," I scowled. It was bad enough Gabe seemed to hate Chase. I couldn't deal with another male attitude.

"He won't listen." My frustration mounted again as I remembered our argument. Of all the things to fight over, we fought about the nativity at church next weekend. Chase was playing the part of Joseph to my Mary, same as we'd done for the last three years. All we had to do is stand in front of our church for two hours Friday and Saturday evening.

Usually only teens participated, but Chase had volunteered two years ago when he came home from college for Christmas break. My boyfriend at the time backed out at the last minute. After that, he just continued to play the part each year. Besides, no one seemed to want the role of Joseph. This was actually the last year I would be participating since I was no longer in high school.

"He wants me to stop being friends with you. Maybe if you two could just—"

The swing jerked to a stop, and Chase came around to stand in front of me. His eyes narrowed, and I could tell he was angry. "Wait a damn minute. What do you mean he told you to stay away from me? Since when does some lowly mechanic have any say in your life? Why are you even talking to him about me?"

"He's not just some mechanic, Chase. He's my boyfriend," I snapped back at him.

Chase stared at me a minute and then shrugged. "So break up with him. You've only been dating, what, two weeks? You don't need someone telling you what to do. You're a big girl."

I laughed, shaking my head at him. "You just told me to break up with him; so technically, you did the same thing he did." I sighed and stared off at the water again, searching for answers. "And we haven't just been dating for two weeks. We've been seeing each other since August, and I love him. What he says, matters to me. I know he's jealous, but I keep telling him you and I are only friends."

Chase turned and walked away to stare at the water. I stared at his back, seeing the tension in his shoulders. Of course, he would be upset. We were good friends. He valued our friendship as much as I did. I watched him as he stooped to pick up several rocks. He threw one at the pond with enough force that it dropped in the middle of the pond, causing the mirrored surface to shatter into a sea of ripples. He continued his onslaught, throwing the rocks until they were gone. He stood, staring at the water with his hands on his hips for a few minutes before finally brushing his palms on his jeans and turning back to me. His eyes were dark and stormy with emotion, but he offered a tight smile, reassuring me that he wasn't angry at me. He walked back to me and touched my cold nose with his finger.

"Come on, Rudolph. Your nose is turning into a cherry," he said quietly.

He pulled me up from the swing and shrugged off his denim jacket, holding it as I slipped my arms inside. I smiled and hugged him. "Thanks, Chase. I'm parked a couple of streets over. Can you give me a ride back to my car?" I asked as we walked to his truck.

He opened the driver's side door for me to slide in across the seat and climbed in after me. He started up the truck and turned up the heat.

My teeth were chattering now. I hadn't I realized how cold I was. My toes were numb, and my face hurt from the cold. He pulled me back across the seat and put his arm around me. He pressed me against his chest and kissed the top of my head.

"Come here so you can warm up," he laughed. "Would you like to come out to the house and say hi to Dad? It's been a while since you've been out, and he misses seeing you. I'll bring you back to your car a little later."

I wasn't ready to talk to Gabe just yet, and I felt guilty; I hadn't visited Chase's dad, Chester, in months. I used to spend a lot of time at the ranch visiting. I smiled up at him and nodded. "Yeah, that would be nice. I'm sorry I haven't been out lately, but with Daddy's surgery and everything." I let my apology trail off, the "everything" being Gabe and his animosity regarding Chase.

He smiled and hugged me to him again. "No sweat. You're coming now, so that's all that matters."

CR ℬ

The tension built inside of me as I got out of my car. I knew what was coming from the furious expressions on my dad and Gabe's faces as they stood on the front porch. It was after nine in the evening--five hours after my promise to be home before dark. Dark was hours ago. I walked slowly up the sidewalk and climbed the steps. Fortunately, they let me get inside the house before tearing into me.

"I can explain," I offered lamely as I pulled Chase's jacket off and tossed it on the coat rack by the door. I flinched as the front door slammed, vibrating the picture frame which hung on the wall beside the door.
"Karsyn Louise McKenna, where the hell have you been?" my father shouted. "Do you have any idea how worried Gabe and I have been about you? We've been out looking for you for hours. What in God's name were you thinking? Gabe found your car on the side of the road, unlocked, and nothing wrong with it. No one could reach you on your phone or had any idea what happened to you. You could have been

36

abducted or something. How would we even know where to start looking for you? Did you even think of that?"

I cringed as the guilt weighed on my shoulders. I should have at least called Dad to let him know where I was. I may have been angry with Gabe, but it wasn't right to worry my dad. He didn't need the stress. I looked at Gabe and felt even worse. He was seething. I turned back to my dad, figuring I'd calm him first. Then I'd deal with my extremely pissed off boyfriend.

"I'm sorry, Daddy. I should have called. Gabe and I had a fight, and I was angry. I needed to clear my head. I didn't mean to worry you. I wasn't thinking. I promise it won't happen again," I swore.

"That's no excuse for your reckless, irresponsible behavior tonight, Kari. You're all I've got, and I can't stand the thought of losing you. I expect better of you than the stunt you pulled today." He stared up at the ceiling taking deep breaths. I felt so much worse when he absently rubbed his chest as if easing pain.

"Daddy, I'm really sorry you were worried. I don't want you to be upset. I swear, I won't take off like that again, ever. I know you're disappointed in me. All I can say is I'm sorry." Tears of shame ran down my face.

He sighed and looked at me. "Unfortunately, you're eighteen now, so I can't very well ground you or punish you. So I guess there's nothing left to say tonight. I need to call the sheriff and let him know you're home."

I watched my dad's retreating form as he walked down the hall to the kitchen. I felt so ashamed. I wiped my eyes and turned to look at Gabe, who had been standing silent. I saw the tick in his jaw and the tense way he held himself, completely closed off to me. He was staring at the jacket hanging beside me.

"Can you forgive me?" I asked softly.

He stared at it another moment before turning his gaze on me. I cringed again at the smoldering rage in his eyes. I should have disintegrated from the intense heat of his expression.

"Where did you get the jacket tonight, Karsyn?" he asked, slowly enunciating each word. "Yours is still in my truck from earlier today." His voice reverberated with anger underneath the deceptively calm tone.

I dropped my gaze to stare at his chest, my guilt making me unable to meet his eyes any longer. I knew how he felt about Chase, however irrational those feelings were.

"You know what? Don't answer that. You and I both know whose jacket that is, don't we? You were with him. While your dad and I drove around town frantic, worrying about you, you were off having a good time with the one man I begged you to stay away from."

I flinched at his accusation, knowing I couldn't deny it. "I'm sorry," I whispered. "Please, Gabe, don't be angry. Chase is my-"

"I've heard it before, Karsyn. You don't need to keep repeating it," he snapped. His voice rose in anger. "Why do you trust him so much? What has he done to earn your blind faith that you will swallow every piece of bullshit he dishes out? Tell me!"

I flinched.

"You say you love me, but yet you can't give me the same fucking level of trust. I tell you to stay away from him, and you won't. I ask you to trust me, and you won't. I beg you to come home so we can talk and work things out, and you run to him. Where is that same loyalty, the same blind faith for me, the man you claim to love?"

I looked up as he stopped to take a breath. He was rubbing his face with his hands. I slipped my arms around his waist and leaned into his chest.

"Please, Gabe. I'm sorry. I love you so much," I begged. "Don't be angry with me."

He sighed and pulled my arms from around him, pushing me away from him. My chest tightened in trepidation. I wanted to turn back the clock to this afternoon and start over. I wouldn't have left the house. I wouldn't have gone with Chase. I wouldn't have worried my dad. I wouldn't be scared I was about to lose Gabe.

"You know what? I can't do this with you right now, Karsyn. I need to get out of here for a while." He grabbed his coat and opened the door.

"Gabe, please don't go," I begged.

He stopped in the entrance and turned to me. "You left earlier today, Karsyn, and wanted me to understand. Well now it's time you gave me the same fucking courtesy."

I dropped to my knees sobbing as the door slammed shut behind him. My stomach churned, and I scrambled to my feet, making it to the bathroom just as I lost my dinner.

Chapter Seven

December 31, 2007

I crawled out of bed feeling slightly less miserable than I had in days. I caught a cold from my day at the park, which then turned into a stomach virus. Between the fevers, runny nose, aches and pains, and vomiting every morning, it had been a rough couple of weeks. Everything was better now, except I still couldn't keep anything down. The smell of meat cooking sent me running for the bathroom faster than if a swarm of bees chased me. I finally broke down and scheduled an appointment with my doctor for this afternoon, hoping she could give me something to stop the nausea.

I avoided Dad as much as possible. Weakened from his heart attack, he developed a mild case of pneumonia just before Christmas and was still fighting it. Plus, I couldn't face his disappointment in me. If we were in the same room, I would catch his look of concern when he thought I wasn't looking.

I missed Gabe. He'd been home for two days, and all I had were his phone calls each day to see how I was and staring at him from my bedroom window as he drove in each morning to the garage and each evening as he left again. We didn't even spend Christmas together. He left town that night after walking out on me. Early the next morning, he called from the airport to reassure me he loved me. He said he didn't want me to think he was leaving me. He explained he was called home and had to leave immediately but promised he was coming back, and we'd talk then.

I had plenty of time to reflect on our fight as I lay in bed or on the bathroom floor between bouts of nausea. While I didn't agree with his feelings about my relationship with Chase, I was ready to admit he had a valid point. How could I say I loved him but not give him my unconditional trust and faith? I didn't want to give up my friendship, but I didn't want to give up the man I loved, either. I decided to make the effort for Gabe. If it was important to him, then I needed to respect his feelings and spend less time with Chase. I wouldn't give up my friendship completely, but I would compromise and limit my interactions. I wanted him to know he was the most important person to me. I was going to give him the same blind faith and trust I gave to Chase.

On Monday, I phoned Chase and told him I needed to distance myself from him for a while for the sake of my relationship with Gabe. He wasn't happy about it but promised to respect my wishes. He said he was willing to put aside whatever differences they had and extend his hand in friendship to Gabe for me. He even offered to invite Gabe wild boar hunting at his lease after the holidays, depending on how things worked out.

I sat on the side of my bed as I debated crawling back in or making a trip to the kitchen in search of anything in the house I could eat, hoping it wouldn't make another appearance within the hour. My phone rang on my bedside table, and I smiled at the caller ID.

"Hi, Gabe." I knew my happy tone traveled through the phone. I stood and walked to my window, looking down to see Gabe getting out of his truck.

"Hi, baby. How are you feeling this morning?" he asked. He looked up at me and waved.

"I'm not sure yet. I haven't tried to eat anything. After I do, I'll let you know." I laughed. "I did make an appointment with my doctor to see if she can prescribe something for the nausea. I just can't seem to shake this bug on my own."

"That's good. I hate that you're sick." He paused a moment. "I miss you, baby. I wish I could make you better."

"I know." I smiled at the wistfulness in his tone. "Hopefully she can give me something, and we'll at least be able to spend New Year's together. I want to give you your Christmas present. It's still under the tree in the living room."

I bought him a new watch for Christmas and had the back engraved with our names and the date of our first kiss.

"I've got something special for you too. I can't wait to give it to you," he whispered.

"Can you give me a clue? Something to get me through until I can see you?" I begged.

He laughed, and I watched him shake his head in amusement. "I tell you what. You go to the doctor today and see what she says. If you're not contagious, then puking or not, you and I are going to spend tonight together." I heard him sigh, and his voice became serious. "Karsyn, I love you more than life. You know that, don't you? I would do anything to make you happy and keep you safe. You're all that matters to me."

"I love you too, Gabe. So much that it hurts. I've done a lot of thinking while I've been sick, and we need to talk." I sighed in frustration. "I don't want to do this over a phone. I swear, Dr. Jamison better say I'm not contagious. I'm coming over tonight even if I have to wear a hazmat suit."

I smiled again when he laughed. "I love you, baby. I gotta get to work. I'll see you tonight. There are some things I need to talk to you about that I couldn't tell you before. If we're going to have a future, then you need to understand everything."

He hung up, and I waved and blew him a kiss from my window. He winked and made the gesture of catching my kiss before blowing one back to me. I watched him walk into the shop to start working and turned to get dressed for another day of lying around the house and recuperating.

My mind drifted to thoughts of seeing Gabe that evening. I missed being in his arms. I couldn't wait to talk to him. I knew he'd be happy that I was putting him first and distancing myself from Chase. I wondered several times what he wanted to tell me. I remembered the conversation I overheard between him and my dad the night he told me he loved me. I had a feeling whatever it was had to be about that. I just wished he would give me a clue. I knew it had to be important.

Gabe called again to check on me after lunch, and we talked a little more. He told me Chase called him at the shop and wanted to meet him for a drink at a club on the highway after work to clear the air. I knew Chase was going to offer but was surprised Gabe agreed so readily to meet. I was hopeful after they talked things would be better between them. He said he'd call me when he got home.

As I was getting dressed for my appointment, I looked out my window to see a red Mustang pull and park in the driveway of the shop. Gabe came outside to greet the person getting out of the car. I was shocked to see Brandi. No one had seen or heard from her since last summer. What was she doing in town now, and why was she here? She'd never used my dad's garage in the past. I shook my head in disbelief; even in the cold, she was dressed in a tight, short, tube dress and spiked high heels. I watched as she talked to Gabe, leaning against her car with her hands propped against the hood behind her. She was flirting with my guy!

I narrowed my eyes, focusing on Gabe's behavior. He was nodding and smiling at whatever she was saying. She stood and ran her finger down his chest, tugging on the waistband of his jeans briefly. Gabe, to his credit, took a step back from her and glanced up at my window. He smiled and waved to me, letting me know he knew I was watching. Brandi turned to see what drew his attention away and gave me a smirk, flipping her long hair off her bare shoulder before turning away again. Gabe opened her car door for her to get in, and she trailed her hand across his chest as she slid into the seat. She drove the car into the garage, hiding from my view. Gabe looked up again and shook his head at me, laughing before following her inside.

CR SO

I sat trying to watch a movie with Dad, waiting for Gabe to call. Dad watched me, concerned at my agitation. I noticed Dad seemed to be on edge all evening as well, constantly looking at the clock. I was too wrapped up in my own head though to give it much thought.

When my phone finally rang, though, it was Chase, not Gabe. He said Gabe had too much to drink, and he just wanted to be sure he got home okay. I told him I already had plans to see Gabe so would drive over and check on him. Before Chase hung up, he assured me they had a good talk and that things were going to be better now.

I hoped Chase was just overreacting about the drinking. Gabe never had more than two beers at any one time. One day last summer, we had been joking around about our most embarrassing moments as part of getting to know each other. I told him about accepting a dare from Heather to moon the entire football team at practice the summer before our senior year. I spent a month washing every car that came to the shop as punishment. I hadn't realized my dad was in the stands watching at the time.

He told me about getting drunk at a cousin's wedding when he was fifteen. His dad had given him permission to have one drink at the reception. A favorite cousin convinced him his dad meant one of every beverage served. He said his dad decided to teach him a lesson. He made him place his new boots on either side of the toilet when he needed to throw up. I didn't understand until he pointed out he was so drunk, he was seeing double and couldn't stand up straight. He threw up inside both shoes, ruining them. I thought that was harsh, but Gabe told me he'd begged for that specific pair of boots for months, so ruining them with his own irresponsible behavior was a valuable lesson. He said it taught him to always keep a clear head so he would never ruin anything that was important to him, and no one would ever be able to convince him to do something so stupid again.

I pulled up to Gabe's house and parked on the street. I wondered why his truck was in the drive instead of the garage where he normally kept it parked. I walked to the front door and was surprised to find it partially open. I knocked and let myself in.

"Gabe!" I called out.

I walked through the living room. Everything was dark, so I turned on a lamp to see. Maybe he did have too much to drink and had already gone to bed even though it was only nine o'clock. I hoped not. I couldn't imagine going home again without sharing my news. I didn't want to wait until tomorrow. I listened for a response. Not getting one, I started down the hall calling his name again. I halted and felt my blood chill when I heard a feminine giggle come from the open doorway at the end of the hall.

"That's it, baby. You like that don't you?" a woman moaned loudly.

I walked with dread down the hall and froze in the doorway of Gabe's room. My heart shattered at the sight before me. Gabe was lying naked in his bed. Straddling his waist was a naked woman, moaning and kissing his chest. As I stared, frozen in shock, my only thought was they were lying in the same bed I'd given him my virginity in. The same bed we'd conceived our child now growing inside of me. I heard the sob rip from my soul.

The woman slowly turned her head around to see me standing there. She smiled and sat up slowly, raking her nails down Gabe's chest.

Brandi.

Of all the people he could have picked, it just had to be her. I felt sick. Every time she'd ever made me feel small and insignificant came rushing back at me. Why her? I would have been hurt no matter whom he cheated on me with, but with Brandi, I was devastated.

"Gabe, baby, you have company," she giggled loudly, keeping her eyes locked on me.

Gabe's eyes cracked open slightly to look at me. I couldn't believe my eyes. He smiled.

"Karsyn? What are you doing here?" He turned to face Brandi as I vaguely registered his slurred speech. He groaned as Brandi ground her hips into his and turned his face to her. "Oh, God, Brandi."

I whimpered and turned, running from the house. I couldn't be there any longer. Brandi's laughter followed me from the house. I stumbled in the yard and fell to my knees, heaving in the grass. I felt hands gently pull my hair back and hold my shoulders. I fought against his grip, crying harder.

"Let me go, you bastard! Get your hands off me!" I screamed through broken sobs.

"It's alright, Karsyn. I've got you, love," a deep voice said gently.

It took a moment for the voice to penetrate my brain and realize it wasn't Gabe who was holding my shaking form. Chase gently lifted me into his strong arms, and I dropped my head against his firm chest. I felt the movement as he walked across the yard with me. I briefly wondered what he was doing here, but at that moment, I only felt gratitude.

Chapter Eight

My sobs had finally died down to the occasional whimper or hiccup. Chase cradled me in his arms as he rocked me gently back and forth in his overstuffed recliner. I absently twisted and shredded the newest tissue he gave me from the half-empty box beside him. Occasionally, I would feel his lips caress my forehead or his fingers run through my hair as he massaged my scalp. I didn't remember the drive to his ranch. I just wanted to close my eyes against the world around me, but when I did, the images came back to me. I whimpered again when Chase's lips pressed against my hair.

"Shhh. I've got you, love. No one will ever hurt you again. I'll take care of you," he whispered.

I smiled sadly at the term of endearment. If only someone did love me enough to make the hurt go away. But no one ever loved me except Dad and Gran. Every one of my boyfriends dumped me, and the man I finally gave my heart to betrayed me. I had no one.

"I need to let my dad know where I am so he doesn't worry." Gabe may have broken every promise he ever made to me, but I would keep my promises.

"You can call him in a little while when you're calmer."

"Thank you." I paused. "Why were you there tonight?"

His fingers stilled before continuing their path through my hair. "He had a few drinks at the bar and was flirting with Brandi. I thought it was harmless at the time. I mean, he's dating you, so why would he be interested in anyone else? I only suggested you go over there in case Brandi showed up. She was all over him at the bar, and I wouldn't put it past her. I figured if you were there, it would let her know he was spoken for and to back off. But after I called you, I got worried. What if the mechanic was interested in her or a violent drunk? I didn't want you to get hurt. I'm so sorry, Karsyn," he replied softly.

"Gabe," I corrected, automatically.

He shifted to look down at me. "Does it really matter anymore, Karsyn, if I say his name or not?" He sighed.

I thought about everything that had happened and shook my head. "No, I guess not. Nothing matters anymore."

We sat silently for a few minutes when a thought occurred to me. "Why do you keep calling me love?"

His hand stopped moving, and I waited for an answer. I tilted my face up to see him staring down at me. There was a vulnerability in his eyes I'd never seen before. Chase was always in control of his world. As I searched his eyes for an answer, my breath hitched at seeing the emotion in his eyes. Love for me. I stared into his eyes, unable to look away as his face came closer to mine. How could I be so blind all this time? How did I not see that Chase felt more than friendship for me? It explained his animosity toward Gabe.

"I called you love because that's what you are. I love you, Karsyn. I have for years. I was only waiting for you to grow up before telling you. It wasn't right before; you were too young," he explained. "I know you don't feel the same way yet, but you will, if you give us a chance."

He leaned in and brushed his lips gently against my own; his fingers softly stroked my cheek. I held myself passively in his arms. I couldn't return his kiss, but I hurt too much to pull away. I wanted him to make the pain go away. I wanted him to be my personal Superman like always and save me from the pain in my heart. My jaw trembled, and I fought the urge to start crying again. These were the wrong lips kissing me. I wanted Gabe's lips to kiss me. But his lips were busy kissing Brandi right now. I gasped in pain at the thought, and Chase raised his head and sighed. He brushed his fingers through my hair again and kissed my forehead.

"I know you're hurt and it's too soon for you, but could you give us a chance, Karsyn? I can make you happy."

I thought about the innocent life growing inside me and shook my head. "Trust me, Chase, you don't want me."

He chuckled deeply and wrapped his arms tighter around me. "How could I not want you? You're everything I've ever wanted."

I swallowed the lump of emotion in my throat. Tonight I lost the man I loved, and I was fixing to lose my best friend with my next words.

"I'm pregnant," I whispered softly. "I found out this afternoon."

I felt him stiffen and I cringed. I could only imagine the disgust I would find in his eyes if I looked up. I was eighteen and knocked up. The father was a cheating bastard. I started to pull away when his arms locked around me.

"I'm sorry, you took me by surprise. That's all." Chase was silent as he processed whatever was going through his mind. "Does he know? Does your dad know yet? Have you told Heather or anyone?"

I shook my head. "No, I wanted to tell Gabe first. I was hoping we'd tell my dad together. I never got the chance. I walked in on—" I couldn't finish the words. The devastation I felt, knowing what I would face alone now in the coming months crushed me beneath its weight. When I left the doctor's office this afternoon, I never imagined this night would play out this way. I started crying again.

"I'm sorry you had to see that. I know it couldn't have been pleasant knowing he cared so little for you to cheat on you with Brandi."

I cowered at his words. I didn't need him to remind me; Gabe obviously didn't love me. "I guess I should get home. I need to talk to Dad and then figure out how I'm going to raise my baby alone." The guilt weighed me down. This would cause Dad even more stress, and he would be disappointed in me again. It seemed that's all I did lately, disappoint my dad.

"How far along are you? Do you know?" Chase asked thoughtfully.

"Dr. Jamison can't be certain until the ultrasound, but she figures I'm about five or six weeks. She thinks I conceived around Thanksgiving."

He was silent for a moment before he spoke again. I could have never guessed his next words

"Marry me, Karsyn." His voice was firm and there was conviction behind his statement.

I looked up in shock and confusion. "Why? I just told you I'm pregnant. Why would you ask me to marry you?"

He sighed, staring at me, and I felt the slight tug in my hair as his fingers twisted around my locks. He shifted so I sat up on his lap, and he cupped my face in his hands. He stared intently into my eyes.

"Marry me, Karsyn. Let me be the father to your baby. No one has to know it isn't mine. First babies are always late, and we can claim it's premature." He placed his hand possessively against my stomach. "Let this child be mine. I promise I will love it as my own because it came from you. Let me spoil you and love you as only I can. I'll love

MICHAEL SCHNEIDER

you enough for both of us until your love grows, as I know it will. I promise you'll never find me in bed with another woman. I'll never need anyone else as long as I have you."

Tears slid down my face at his words. I shook my head at him. "I can't do that to you, Chase. It wouldn't be fair."

"Is it fair that you gave yourself to another man who didn't love you the way I do? Is it fair that you're now carrying the burden of that mistake? Is it fair to dump this on your father, knowing it will hurt him?" His voice tinged in anger rose steadily with each question.

I let my gaze shift to stare unseeing across the room. I couldn't face him any longer. I cringed at the truth of his words. I didn't want to burden my father with the stress of worrying about an unwed pregnant daughter. I couldn't, wouldn't face Gabe after what he did tonight. It would be too painful, and I knew every time I looked at him, I would see the image of him in bed with her. Where else could I turn, if not to Chase?

He paused in his tirade and sighed. He kissed my forehead and stroked my hair softly as he captured my gaze again. Love and compassion filled his eyes. "You can't do this alone, Karsyn," he warned me quietly. "I promise to love you and cherish you as you deserve. I can make you happy, if you'll let me."

"Are you sure this is what you want?" I asked hesitantly. "Can you really love my baby even though it wouldn't be yours?"

"This child is part of the woman I have loved for so long. I will watch it grow inside of you, and I'll be there when it's born. My name will be on the birth certificate, making the baby mine to the outside world. We can have more children so this baby has little brothers and sisters running around. I want our home filled with the sounds of children laughing and playing. Something you and I never had. I want to buy

52

him a pony and teach him to ride and shoot a rifle. I'll take him hunting and fishing."

I laughed in amusement at the picture he painted. "And what if it's a girl? What are you going to do then?"

He kissed the top of my head, obviously happy I was at least considering his proposal. "Well then, if it's a girl, she'll be just as beautiful as her mommy, and I will love her all the more for it. She'll be Daddy's little princess, and I'll build her a castle behind the house. She'll wear frilly dresses, and I'll spoil her rotten. She'll be the happiest little girl in the world. All it takes is for you to say yes. Make my every dream come true," he proclaimed.

I stilled at the thought that not every dream of mine would come true. The dream of being Gabe's wife would never come true. Tonight was supposed to be about creating these same plans and dreams for our future, our baby. It was his arms that should be holding me, comforting me, reassuring me that, although this baby wasn't planned, everything would be fine. Those dreams were gone now; shattered by his unfaithfulness, never to be restored.

I thought about his proposal. If I married Chase, I wouldn't have to tell my father of my disgrace. I wouldn't face the sympathetic stares of people in town. My baby would have two parents, something I never had. And if I allowed myself one vindictive thought, it would be a way to get back at Gabe for what he'd done. Gabe hates Chase, so to see me married to the one man he absolutely can't stand would be the perfect payback. I refused to listen to my subconscious telling me this wasn't right.

"You're really sure, Chase? Because I don't think I can handle having my heart broken again. I'm sorry I can't love you like you love me right now. But if you're sure, then I promise to spend every day being the best wife I can."

He stood and put me back down in his recliner, walking to a picture on the wall. I watched as he swung the frame away from the wall, revealing a safe behind. He spun the combination and opened the door. He picked something up from inside before closing it again and coming back to me. He knelt on one knee in front of me and opened a small velvet box.

"This ring belonged to my mother, and I saved it with the hope of one day putting it on your finger." He opened the lid to reveal a magnificent ring. Diamonds surrounded a large pear-shaped ruby in the center. The wide band was made of white and yellow gold. "My mother loved rubies, and she and Dad were married in July. Unfortunately we can't wait for a summer wedding, but your birthstone is the diamond and mine is the ruby, so it still fits for us."

He reached up to wipe away my tear, which slid down my face, capturing it with his thumb. "Karsyn Louise McKenna, please say you'll be my wife? I promise to do everything in my power to ensure another sad tear never falls from your eyes again. Let me be your Superman for as long as we live."

I sobbed at his beautiful proposal and nodded as he slid the ring on my left hand. He pulled me up and swung me around in his arms, whooping loudly. I laughed at seeing how happy he was and vowed he would never regret marrying me. He kissed me again, and this time I worked to put everything I could into returning his kiss. It still hurt and felt wrong, but I'd given my promise, so now I needed to make it work.

"I need to go home," I said when he put me back down. He was still cupping my face in his hands, feathering me with kisses.

"No, I'm not letting you go. Not even for a minute," he growled. "You're all mine, now."

I laughed at his possessiveness and then sighed, pushing against his chest to release me. "Chase, I need to tell my dad what's going on. I don't want him to worry."

He continued to hold me, refusing to let me go for even a moment. He stared at me, and I could almost see the wheels turning in his head. He was always planning and thinking.

"I'm taking you to Vegas tonight. I'll call and have my private jet ready by the time we get to the airport. We can be married tomorrow. I can't think of a better way to ring in the New Year than with you as my bride. We'll pick up Heather on the way to come with us. I know you would want her with you. We can call your dad on the way. Tell him you're going out of town for a few days and will be back soon."

I shook my head, laughing at him. In just a couple of minutes, he had everything worked out. He was always like that. Whatever obstacle was in his path, he seemed to have a plan in place for removing it. I realized sadly, that by saying yes to a Vegas wedding with Chase, I was giving up my dream of my father walking me down the aisle. Tonight I seemed to be giving up a lot of my dreams.

෬ ෭

"Daddy, he cheated on me! I saw him with my own eyes! He was in bed with Brandi," I cried.

We were in the air on the way to Las Vegas. I was standing in the galley, trying to talk to Dad. Heather was asleep on the leather sofa. I couldn't believe my father was trying to convince me to come home and talk to Gabe after what he did. I would think he would want to kill Gabe for what he'd done to me. How could he expect me to be okay with everything?

"Kari, just come home. There are things you don't know. Let us just explain," Dad begged. "Do not go anywhere with Chase Carter!"

Chase stood behind me holding me in his arms. His chin rested on my shoulder where I was holding the phone to my ear. He heard my dad through the phone, and I was embarrassed.

"Daddy, how can you take Gabe's side against your own daughter?" I snapped.

"Kari, Gabe is an und-"

I looked up as Chase took my cell phone from me. He kissed the top of my head as he listened to whatever my dad had been saying to me. He glanced down and put his hand over the phone.

"Go rest, love. We have a busy day ahead of us. I'll finish talking to your dad."

I nodded and walked back to my seat. As I walked away, I heard Chase speak to my dad.

"Hello, Carson." He paused, chuckling at whatever my dad was saying. "Yes, well Karsyn is my concern, now. I promise she'll be home soon." He met my gaze and winked. "Good-bye, Carson. Thanks for everything. You and the mechanic have a pleasant night."

Chapter Nine

We landed in Las Vegas in the early morning hours. A limousine waited to take us to our hotel. Chase booked the three of us into a double suite at one of the casinos on the Strip. I was too tired and emotionally drained to pay attention to which one. They all blurred together in a sea of blinding lights anyway. Chase carried me through our suite and tucked me into the huge bed, telling me to sleep while he took care of all the details.

When I woke hours later, I found several garment bags hanging in the closet with various designer names stamped on them. Boxes of shoes lined floor and shopping bags covered the small loveseat by the window. Surprised, I briefly wondered how I would carry everything back home with me until I spied a new set of Louis Vuitton luggage.

Curiosity got the better of me, and I got up to see what was in all the bags. When I picked up a lacy thong, I flushed in embarrassment at the thought of Chase picking out panties for me to wear. Among all the clothing, I found a small, white, paper bag that rattled when I shook it. I opened it to reveal a bottle of pre-natal vitamins. I slumped to the floor, and the tears began as I hugged the bottle to my chest.

As I stared at the vitamins in my hands, I remembered the past. The first time I noticed Chase was at my father's garage, I was fourteen, and he'd come with his father to discuss their contract. He was so handsome and serious at nineteen, learning the ropes as he prepared for the day he would take over his father's businesses. A few months later when he rescued my kitten from the vending machine, he became my personal hero. He and his father came to Gran's funeral, and he held me while I cried. I spent weekends at his ranch, horseback riding and hanging out when his father would invite my dad to go hunting or fishing. I remembered my junior year in high school when my boyfriend dumped me after the homecoming game in the parking lot just before the dance. Chase offered to take me instead. He was home from college for the weekend and had come to the game. I didn't know he was standing nearby to witness my breakup. He danced with me all night and told me jokes and stories about his family. Chase had always been there for me—my personal Superman. I knew, looking at the bottle in my hands, he would continue to be there for me and for my child.

Now I could see the love he'd kept hidden from me while he waited for me to grow up. Well, I was growing up very quickly now. In one day, I'd experienced heartbreak and betrayal, found out I was pregnant, and was getting married; I figured it didn't get more grown up than that.

I looked up at the sound of the bedroom door opening and smiled.

"Hey," I called, drawing her attention to where I was still sitting on the floor.

"Oh, my God! Can you believe we're spending New Year's in Vegas? I wish we were twenty-one so we could go to the casinos," Heather gushed. "Oh, and since when do you keep secrets from me? Chase told me what a slime ball Gabe is. I can't believe he would cheat on you with that skank. They must have been sleeping together for months. I mean she doesn't even live in town anymore, so how else would they know each other unless they were sleeping together?"

My hands clenched tightly and I took a deep steadying breath. I would not cry again over Gabe. Blinking rapidly, I fought my traitorous tears that refused to cooperate with my decision.

"Good riddance, I say. I'm glad you're marrying Chase. You make a cute couple, and I knew Chase had a thing for you. I saw the emotion he tried to hide every time he looked at you." She leaned down to pull me up and push me to the bathroom, grabbing the bag of toiletries along the way.

"Come on. You need a shower. Someone from the hotel salon is coming to help us get ready. Chase said we have two hours. He's sending a limo to pick us up and take us to the chapel to meet him. I can't wait 'til you see the dress he bought you. Oh, my God! It's freaking gorgeous! And you should see mine! Fabulous!"

I laughed, shaking my head at Heather. She rarely gave you a chance to speak once she started. At least I wouldn't need to answer any questions. Heather chattered while the salon consultant pampered us with manicures and pedicures, styled our hair, and did our makeup. Chase took Heather her shopping with him while I slept, which eased my mind that Chase did not pick out the white lacey thong I was currently wearing.

CR   SO

I stepped out of the limousine and looked up at the entrance to the chapel. I stared at the heavy oak doors flanked on either side by stained-glass windows. I should have known Chase would make our wedding special, no matter how short the notice. There would be no typical Vegas wedding with Elvis impersonators performing the ceremony or plastic hearts and cherubs adorning the walls. No, we would be married in an actual church with an actual minister, making our union more real. The only thing missing today was my father to walk me down the aisle and the pews filled with family and friends. Another dream I lost because of Gabe's cheating. All of this was his fault.

It still seemed unreal how much my life changed in such a short time. Chase was the man waiting for me inside, not the man I dreamed of marrying just days ago. That dream was laid to rest with all my childish fantasies of storybook happy endings.

Heather left me in the vestibule while she went to let Chase know we'd arrived. She said the music would queue my entrance in a few minutes. I turned to stare at the mirror hanging on the wall. It wasn't my reflection, but that of a stranger. This person was sophisticated and beautiful. She bore no resemblance to the eighteen-year-old girl from yesterday. Her heavy locks were curled and pinned up at her crown with a wisp of veil falling down her back. Her dress of white satin had tiny delicate straps holding up the bodice covered in lace and beading. The satin clung to her curves falling to a short train. I didn't know this woman.

How had my life gone so wrong so fast? What had I done or not done to alter the outcome of events so drastically? Was I too young, too naïve to be enough for Gabe? Was I not a good enough daughter for my father that he chose to make excuses for Gabe rather than protect me? The only one I had left to lean on was Chase. He loved me and was willing to open his heart to another man's child. No greater gift could he ever give me than that.

The organ began to play, and I turned away from the mirror, ready to make a new life and new dreams.

❧ ☙

I nervously twisted the rings on my finger as I stared out the window of our room. I was now Mrs. Chester Carter IV, Karsyn Carter. Karsyn McKenna no longer existed. I heard the door close and the rustle of clothing behind me indicating Chase, my husband, was in the room. My breath hitched as he came to stand behind me.

"Heather said good-bye, and she'll see you in six weeks. The limo just picked her up," he said. "I told her not to tell her parents about the wedding when she talks to them because we want to tell your father first when we get back." He kissed my shoulder as he handed me a champagne flute.

"Thank you. The trip is extremely thoughtful and generous. I know she'll have a great time," I replied. I hated the way my voice squeaked, betraying my nerves.

As a thank you gift to Heather for dropping everything to be here for me, Chase booked her on a Hawaiian cruise with a month stay to island hop before boarding another cruise back home. He also gave her a credit card with carte blanche usage for any shopping she may want to do on her trip.

I lifted the flute to my lips and then stopped, remembering I was pregnant.

"It's just sparkling cider," he explained with a soft chuckle.

I couldn't help the smile at his thoughtfulness but wished for something stronger to help me in this moment. I was nervous about what was to come.

"Have I told you how much I love you, Mrs. Carter, and how beautiful you are?" he said softly.

His arms wrapped around me, pulling me against his hard chest. He didn't seem to expect any response from me, for which I was grateful. I didn't trust my voice in that moment. He kissed my shoulder again, and I tilted my head as his lips left a moist trail on my skin on their path to my ear. I heard the rasp of my zipper lowering and stiffened, closing my eyes against the sudden sting of tears. My lip trembled as I felt his hands remove the pins, which held my veil in place. His fingers gently massaged my scalp before smoothing my hair down my back.

"Chase, I—" I began hesitantly. I could hear the tremor in my voice. I was scared. I wasn't ready for this. Gabe is the only man I'd ever been with. No! I refused to think about him tonight of all nights.

"Shhh, love. It's alright. I won't hurt you. I just want to make love to my bride. You have no idea how long I've dreamed of this night, Karsyn. Let me take care of you." He took the flute from my stiff fingers.

His words were meant to reassure me, yet I couldn't face him and kept my eyes closed. I tried to still my rapidly beating heart. His fingers scraped against my shoulders as he pulled the straps of my gown down my arms. The soft material rushed past my legs and pooled at my feet. Lifting me in his arms, he carried me across the room and laid me on the cool softness of the bed. There was a tug at my hips as he slid my thong down my legs, leaving me bare to his perusal. A tear escaped from the corner of my still closed eyes.

"Open your eyes, Karsyn," he demanded softly. "Look at me."

The bed dipped from his weight, and I opened my eyes slowly to see him sitting beside me. I'd never seen his eyes look so intense before. A fire raged in the depths of his gaze as his eyes gazed into me. Another tear slid from the corner of my eye to leave a trail of wetness to my hair, and then another swiftly followed. His hungry gaze swept over me before locking again with mine. My hand moved automatically to shield me from his view, but he reached out, capturing my wrist and placing it back on the bed beside me. He watched the silent tears flow from my eyes for a moment before brushing away the trail with his thumb.

He sighed and leaned down kissing a tear, which still clung to the corner of my eye.

"Karsyn, if you're not ready for this, we can wait. We have the rest of our lives to make love." I heard the compassion and love in his voice, tinged with disappointment.

"I promise I want this, Chase. Please." I let my plea dangle in the air for him to take whatever meaning from it. I didn't know what I was really pleading for. I wasn't ready, but I needed to erase Gabe. I needed Chase to make me forget the hurt.

He moved to place a gentle kiss on my lips. I knew he felt them tremble. He stood and began unbuttoning his stark white shirt, pulling it from the waistband of his black slacks. I watched as he removed his belt and pants. I needed to see that he was the man who would make love to me tonight. He was the man I pledged myself to. Whatever was left of my dreams with Gabe would be erased tonight.

I kept my eyes focused on his as he moved back to slide into the bed beside me. I tried to reach for the blanket to cover me, us, but he wouldn't allow it. He tugged the cover from my grasp and tossed it to the foot of the bed.

"You're not cold, Karsyn. You're just nervous," he admonished gently. "I would never hurt you. I'm your husband. You're my wife. I want you to keep your eyes open when I make love to you tonight. I want you to see how much I love and cherish you."

He leaned down, and my breathing hitched as his lips pressed into my stomach below my naval. He rose over me and shifted to nestle between my legs. He pressed kisses to my stomach and stroked his fingers soothingly over and around my abdomen as he whispered words of love to the life growing inside me. Occasionally he would lift his eyes to mine as I watched. He would smile and go back to focusing on my—no, our—child. As I watched him focus on my stomach, my trembling eased. Resolve settled over me; I would do everything in my power to make our marriage work, beginning tonight.

I slowly lifted my hand to run my fingers through his hair. I rubbed the strands, familiarizing myself with the texture. His hair was thick but coarse, different from—I didn't allow myself to complete that thought. I continued to rake my fingers across his scalp as I calmed further. His eyes lifted to study my face. I nodded my head to his silent question. My hands settled to rest on his shoulders as he slid back up the bed to lie on top of me. I felt his chest against my breasts and the evidence of his arousal on the inside of my thigh. He held himself above me, brushing my hair back from my face as his eyes studied mine.

I slid my hands hesitantly up his shoulders to the back of his head and pulled him down, opening my mouth to his. His tongue slid into my mouth, and I touched his tentatively with mine. It was all the encouragement he needed before he took over and dominated our kiss. I felt the tug against my scalp as his hands fisted in my hair, holding my head immobile as he plundered my mouth. I raked my nails across his shoulders and upper back, and I felt him shudder. His lips released mine, and he left a trail of heated kisses down the side of my neck and across my collarbone, before dipping down to capture my nipple between his lips. I held his head to my breast and released a quiet moan as the first embers of desire sparked within me. He continued to lathe attention on my breasts, and when he finally slid one hand down to my soft curls below, he found me ready for his touch.

When Chase raised his face from my breast and stared into my eyes, I pushed all thoughts about why I was doing this out of my head to live in the moment. His fingers continued to stroke me, and my back arched, suddenly needing more. I could see the passion he fought to control and the satisfaction he felt that my eyes were open and smoldering with desire for him. He continued to watch my face as he brought me closer, reaching for that special place inside that would shatter me. When my climax came, he captured my lips in a searing kiss and slid his length in me in the same breath.

"You're mine now, Karsyn. Always," he growled.

There was possessiveness in his tone as he held me in his fierce embrace. He was claiming me. He pulled my leg up to wrap around his waist as he drove us toward another climax. I heard Chase's roar of satisfaction as I felt his release deep inside me.

My eyes shut tightly, and I bit my tongue to keep from crying out. I was afraid I would scream the wrong name. That's when everything suddenly crashed down on me.

Oh, God. What have I done? Tears slid into my hairline as I realized the ramifications of my actions. I married Chase. I made love with Chase. I agreed to let Chase claim Gabe's baby as his own. Gabe would never know he was a father. I made my decision in the heat of the moment and couldn't take it back now. I was so hurt and angry from Gabe's betrayal that I made a life altering decision without taking time to really think what it would mean to me, to my baby.

Chase rolled onto his back, bringing me with him and tucked me into his side. I looked over to see him staring at the ceiling, a satisfied smile on his face. He looked at me and hugged me tighter to him, kissing my brow.

"Get some rest, love. Tomorrow we leave for our honeymoon," he laughed softly.

Chase married me knowing I didn't love him and was pregnant with another man's baby. He had always been my best friend and was there for me. He was sweet and kind and, for whatever reason, he loved me. I needed to stop crying over spilt milk as Gran always said. What's done is done. It was time to live with my decision. I needed to show him I was committed to our marriage; that things wouldn't be one-sided between us. I wanted to make him feel as loved as he had just made me feel, even if I couldn't say the words. I took a breath and felt my resolve settle over me as I sat up. I threw my leg over his waist to straddle him and leaned down to kiss his chest, surprising him. I nipped playfully at his collarbone and neck before kissing his lips.

"I'm not done with you yet, Mr. Carter. Mrs. Carter is just getting started."

Chapter Ten

February 3, 2008

We spent a month in Belize for our honeymoon. Chase explained that because his father invested in sugar, his family kept a home there, so they had a place to stay when conducting business with the growers in the area. His associates insisted on throwing a party to celebrate our wedding. They were all so welcoming. I was relieved they spoke English, albeit with a heavy accent. I made friends with a couple of the younger wives; their air of sophistication impressed me.

Listening to Chase converse fluently in Spanish was sexy, and I insisted he teach me since I misunderstood so much of what they were saying. Two years of Spanish in high school, and I only remembered how to count to twenty and a few basic words like eye, chair, and door. I came home early from shopping one day and interrupted his visit with friends. I thought they were discussing beverages and offered to bring everyone something to drink. Chase wrapped me in his arms, laughing, and made me promise never to change.

We toured all the sights, played in the ocean, and made love on the private beach. I couldn't get over the tropical beauty of the area. I wished we could stay forever. Chase promised to bring me back any time I wanted.

I began falling in love with my husband during our stay. I saw him through new eyes as each morning I awoke wrapped in his arms and fell asleep each night sated and cherished in those same arms. He showed me every day that he also loved our child. When we rested during the heat of the day, he would lay beside me with his face nestled against the baby bump I now had. He would talk to my stomach and press warm kisses against it. When I laughed at him, he told me he was teaching our baby to know his voice so it would know his daddy. I always had to fight the tears, which threatened to come when he said this, because another face would always come to mind. I wondered if he even noticed that I'd left. God, when I would stop thinking about him.

When we arrived home from our honeymoon, it was to the news that vandals had burned my dad's garage on the day of our wedding. He was in the hospital in intensive care after being found beaten behind the shop. Chase drove us to the hospital to find out my father's condition. While the news angered Chase, I was just worried. My guilt weighed heavily on me. I didn't call once during our honeymoon. I had felt so betrayed that he wanted me to talk to Gabe after seeing him with Brandi. The last words spoken to my dad were in anger. Did I even tell him I loved him? I prayed I would still get the opportunity to do so. I couldn't understand why someone would want to hurt him. He was honest and hardworking. He was a friend to everyone in town, always willing to give the benefit of the doubt, even to the man who betrayed me.

I sat, stunned, as I listened to the surgeon discuss his condition. My brain registered phrases like "drug induced coma," "permanent nerve damage," "months of therapy." The only good news was he wasn't in the garage when it burned. The surgeon told us his injuries were severe because he was still recovering from his previous back surgery and heart attack. The immediate concern was that he hadn't fully recovered from his bout of pneumonia during the holidays. Everything was working against him.

I was never more grateful for Chase's strength than I was now as he handled the discussion of my father's care with the doctor. He demanded the hospital fly in any specialist necessary, sparing no expense to ensure a full recovery. I felt his arm slide protectively around my waist as he guided me from the office and down the hall. The nurse on duty directed us to my father's room.

I wasn't prepared for the sight of Dad's broken body lying so still. He had a breathing tube in his mouth and was hooked up to so many machines; he seemed to be a mass of wires. With his head and neck immobilized and his face a patchwork of cuts and bruises, I found it hard to see the man he was before I left. His arms were in casts, and I noticed several fingers had splints coming out of the cast; his attackers had even broken his fingers. I couldn't even hold his hand. I saw the bulk of the cast on his right leg under his blanket. It didn't help when the nurse assured me that he looked much better than when he came in. He looked more like a car accident victim.

Chase's hands guided me, and just as my legs buckled, I heard the scrape of chair legs and found myself sitting. I leaned against him and cried as he stroked my head soothingly.

"I'm going to step out to give you some time with your dad. I want to call the sheriff and see what he knows. I'll bring you something to eat and drink from the cafeteria."

I nodded my head, unable to speak through the emotions. I felt his lips press against the top of my head and heard him sigh. He kneeled down beside me and cupped my face in his hands, turning me to look at him. I saw the concern in his eyes when he looked at me. I pressed my face into his hand, wanting his comfort.

"Karsyn, I promise you, the ones who did this will be punished," he vowed. "Your dad shouldn't be in this condition. He will have the best care money can buy."

His thumbs brushed away the tears spilling down my cheeks. He drew me to him and kissed me gently. When he pulled away, he gave me a reassuring smile and placed his hand on my stomach. "He's going to get through this. He's tough and he's strong. He's going to be around to bounce our children on his knee. Don't get discouraged."

My lips trembled as I tried to smile at the thought of my dad playing with our children. I held onto that image to give me hope. "Have I told you today how much I love you?" I whimpered.

He smiled and leaned in to kiss me again. "I love you, too. I want you to stay right here in this room. I'll be back in just a few minutes," he stressed.

I nodded and as he left, turned back to Dad. I pulled my chair closer to the bed and stroked his upper arm, the only place on him that didn't look like it was hurt. I laid my head on the side of his bed and stared absently at the machine monitoring his pulse and blood pressure. I heard the door open a few minutes later. I didn't bother acknowledging the person who entered. It would be either a nurse or Chase.

"Karsyn?"

I tensed, recognizing the voice. I shut my eyes, wishing him away. I didn't want to see him. He shouldn't be here.

"Karsyn, baby? Please tell me I'm not dreaming, and you're really here," he begged.

He pulled me from my chair, and he held my face in his hands, staring desperately at me. He leaned his head back and laughed in what sounded like relief before wrapping me in a fierce embrace. He rained kisses over my face as he whispered words of love to me. His lips felt so right on my skin. I remembered how perfectly I fit within his arms. How could this still feel so right? I was married to another man. I battled with my body not to respond and clenched my fists at my side to keep from hugging him. He had no right to hold me now. I wasn't his any longer and he wasn't mine.

He held me at arm's length; his gaze sweeping over me like a thirsty man in the desert looks at a glass of water. I let my eyes soak him in. If I was honest with myself, I was just as hungry for him. I wished again that things were different. I knew no matter what I was beginning to feel for Chase, it would never match the all-consuming fire I felt for Gabe. No matter what he'd done, I just couldn't stop loving him. He would always be my true love.

"How did you get away? Do you know where he held you? We searched all over Hawaii for you, but no one recognized you from the photo at any of the hotels you were booked. I need to get you out of here. You're not safe."

His rapid-fire questions and comments made no sense. I stared at him in confusion. I began to take notice of the tired lines and dark circles around his eyes. His clothes looked like he'd slept in them, more than once. Something wasn't right. I could always tell when he was stressed or worried as he was now. I wanted to soothe the worry lines on his brow. I had to remind myself that he wasn't mine to worry about any longer.

"What are you talking about?" I asked as I tried to pull away.

He pulled me tighter to him. I heard him hiss into my hair. "God, what he must have put you through. I swear I'll kill him."

I shook my head, confused. I decided it really didn't matter what he was talking about as the image of him and Brandi popped in my head. I reminded myself again that he wasn't mine to worry about. Someone else worried about him now. I stiffened and backed away from him, putting myself out of reach.

"How's Brandi?" I asked harshly.

He sighed heavily and stepped toward me. I took a step back, raising my hands in front of me to stop him. He sighed again.

"It wasn't what it looked like," he started.

My laugh was hollow. I knew I was holding on by a thread. I loved Chase, but I was doomed to always love Gabe, especially with the child I carried. The images of that night flashed through my mind like on a loop.

"Really? I may not have a lot of experience, but when you're lying naked in bed with a naked woman straddling your hips, it looks like sex. I wasn't aware that you were just having your book club meeting," I sneered. "My mistake. That must be what you and Brandi discussed in my dad's garage that afternoon, too. What book you were going to read together later? At your house. In your bed. With no clothes on."

"Karsyn, baby. He set me up," he said as if that explained everything. He reached for me again, this time catching my elbow, pulling me back into his arms as I struggled against him. "I promise I'll explain everything later. We should have never kept you in the dark. Right now I need to get you somewhere safe."

"Well, well. If it isn't the mechanic. I figured you would have cut your losses by now and left town. I told you; you can't win."

I turned to see Chase standing in the doorway. He set down the plate and cup he had with him on the counter. I tugged again, trying to get Gabe to release me. His grip tightened on my arms, and I whimpered in pain. Chase's eyes narrowed and he shot Gabe an ugly look.

"Take your hands off of my wife," he growled.

"Your wife?" Gabe's voice rose in disbelief. His gaze swung to me, his eyes searching mine. I managed to pull away in his distraction and ran to Chase, who wrapped me safely in his arms. I closed my eyes, sobbing. I knew I was crying for the heartbreak I felt at seeing Gabe.

Torn between my love for him and my loyalty to Chase as his wife, would my heart ever give me peace? Chase whispered soothing words of comfort to me. After a moment, he turned his attention back to Gabe.

"That's right. My wife. I'm sorry you weren't invited to the wedding, but I'm sure you understand. It just didn't seem appropriate at the time."

I opened my eyes as Chase tilted my chin up to look at him. "Are you alright, love?" he asked gently.

I nodded, unable to respond through my broken sobs.

His eyes cut to Gabe, and a look flashed in them. It was gone so quickly, I couldn't name it. He kissed my brow as his hand slid down to settle low on my stomach.

"I want you to see the doctor before we leave. Stress isn't good for your condition," he reminded me gently. His voice carried, and I knew Gabe heard. I cringed at his words. I didn't owe Gabe anything, but still, it wasn't fair for him to find out this way. If I was honest, I hoped he'd never know. It wasn't fair for Chase to flaunt my pregnancy in front of Gabe knowing it was his baby I carried.

Gabe's eyes widened in shock and then narrowed to settle on me. Chase smoothed his hand over my stomach as he watched. I knew Gabe would be able to see the slight baby bump through my snug sweater dress. I wanted to rush to explain everything, but I couldn't. My scalp crawled, and I felt the chill slide down my spine at the ugly look that came over Gabe's face when he finally looked back up to stare at me.

His mouth opened and closed several times before his jaw clenched. His hands curled into fists at his side. When he finally spoke, it was with dead calm.

"Let me get this straight. You ran off and married this bastard and got yourself knocked up with his brat while your father lay here fighting for his life?" he sneered. His finger pointed accusingly at me. "I've been searching for you for a month!" he yelled. "You aren't the person I thought you were, Karsyn. I hope you'll be very happy playing house with this monster. You really have no idea what you've done, do you? Your father is going to be so disappointed in you when he finds out."

His gaze cut to Chase. "I still have a job to do, so don't think this is the end."

He turned and stalked away. He turned back to me as he opened the door. His gaze swept over me with Chase's arms wrapped around me as my tears continued, pausing on my stomach for a brief moment. He looked at Chase and then sneered at me.

"I'll have to look Brandi up. Maybe we can finish that book we started." With that, he turned and walked out, letting the door slam behind him. It was as if the door had slammed on my heart. I wished again that things had happened differently. No matter the hurt he caused me, I couldn't stop loving him. I feared I always would.

Chapter Eleven

January 1, 2009

Tonight we celebrated our one-year anniversary with dinner at home. Abby had a case of the sniffles, and I didn't want to leave her or take her out in the cold. Justin, Heather, and her parents came to help celebrate. Dad was here as well but refused to share in the toast.

When Dad first came out of the coma, he blamed Chase for his injuries. I tried to get my father to see reason. Chase paid all his medical bills. Why would he do that if he wanted him hurt? It didn't make sense. Dad spent two months in the hospital and another seven months in physical therapy. He still had trouble with numbness in his fingers and would always walk with a limp.

Dad's constant animosity toward Chase in the beginning began to wear on me. Chase gently reminded me that my father suffered a concussion, and combined with the pain medications he was taking; it may have affected his personality.

I ended up in the emergency room after a particularly bad argument caused my blood pressure to spike dangerously. Chase put his foot down. If my father wanted to be a part of my life and his grandchild's, then he would have to stop saying things that upset me. If not, he would cut off all contact between us. I was Chase's first priority. My dad and I weren't as close as we once were, and that bothered me, but we were trying.

I couldn't believe Heather and Justin were still dating. This was the longest relationship she'd ever been in. She'd even moved in with him before the holidays, so things were pretty serious. They met eight months ago after Justin pulled out in front of her, causing an accident. He offered to pay for her damages out of pocket instead of filing a claim and threw in dinner as an added incentive. Before long, they were a couple and coming out to the ranch for barbeques. It didn't hurt that Justin and Chase were now friends, too.

Our first year together had been full of ups and downs, but tonight's celebration reminded us it was well worth it. After Heather's parents left, taking my dad with them, Heather, Justin, Chase, and I discussed our plans to take them with us to Belize next month. Chase and I had made a couple of trips there for his business. This time Justin and Heather were coming with us for a vacation.

"I can have Mrs. Murphy watch Abby for me next Saturday, so you and I can go shopping and have lunch," I said. "We can eat at that little restaurant you told me about."

"Oh, that reminds me. You'll never guess who I saw last week. Gabe," Heather gushed. She turned to Justin, interrupting his quiet conversation with Chase from across the room. "You remember? The guy you ran into on the sidewalk when I came to surprise you for lunch?"

I tensed at his name and closed my eyes to shut out the sudden pain in my heart. I loved Chase. He was a wonderful husband to me and a good father to Abby, but hearing Gabe's name still caused me pain. I looked at Chase, who had stilled at the news. Justin seemed embarrassed.

"Honestly, no I don't remember. I'm sorry, but why would I?" he shrugged. "He was just some guy on the street."

He turned to Chase. "I apologize, Chase. I think that last drink got to Heather."

He frowned at Heather. "It's a little tacky, Heather, to bring up your friend's ex-boyfriend on her anniversary."

Heather turned to me, wide-eyed. "Oh, Karsyn, I'm so sorry. I didn't even think. Me and my big mouth. Forget I said anything. Besides, it looked like he was meeting Brandi. She was getting out of a taxi when we left." She slapped her hand over her mouth. "Crap. I did it again." She quickly leaned in, kissed my cheek, and stood. "Okay, we're going to just go before I say anything else stupid tonight." She ran over and hugged Chase, kissing his cheek, also. "Please don't hate me, Chase. I'm sorry. You know I think you're the best."

Chase returned her hug and laughed. "I could never hate you, Heather. Karsyn loves you."

He turned to Justin, who was staring at Heather with irritation and worry, and shook his hand. "Don't worry about it. I'm used to Heather. I promise we'll talk more, later."

Chase was quiet as he helped me straighten the downstairs. When I came back into the living room after cleaning the kitchen, he was staring at the dying embers in the fireplace, poking absently at the logs. I slipped my arms around his waist and rested my cheek against his spine. He put the iron poker back in its holder and turned to wrap me in his arms.

"Chase," I began.

He tilted my face up and kissed me softly. "Don't worry about it. I'm fine," he assured me. "Why don't you go take a shower. I'll be up in a little while. I've got some work to do in my office."

I sighed. "Chase. Please don't be mad at Heather. Come to bed."

He leaned down and captured my lips in a searing kiss. I felt my knees weaken, and my heart speed up before he released me. He chuckled at the desire I knew he saw in my hooded eyes as I stared at his lips, wanting more. "I promise I'm not mad at Heather. I just need to take care of some things. I'll be up by the time you get out of the shower. Maybe we can recreate our wedding night. What do you say, Mrs. Carter?"

"I would like that very much, Mr. Carter."

ႚ ႛ

I turned off the bathroom light and walked into the bedroom. My eyes immediately went to the empty bed and sighed in disappointment. I had hoped he would be here, so I could show off my new negligee I bought for our anniversary. I smiled when I heard rustling and a soft whisper coming from the monitor beside the bed. I tiptoed down the hall to the next room and paused in the doorway. The sight always filled my heart. Chase was sitting in the rocking chair, holding Abby and whispering words of love against her soft hair.

Abigail Lynn Carter was born on September 5, 2008 at three in the morning—one week late—weighing in at eight pounds, three ounces, and twenty-one inches long. I was in labor for seventeen hours. Chase stayed with me the whole time, feeding me ice chips, rubbing my lower back, and letting me crush his hand through each contraction. His constant words of encouragement kept me going when I grew tired and emotional. It was the only time I'd allowed myself to think of someone else and regret; to wish Gabe were with me, holding my hand and helping me bring our child into the world.

No one believed Abby was premature due to her size. The rumor going around was that I'd cheated on Gabe while he was out of town and was pregnant with Chase's baby, explaining our quick wedding. Funny, how accurate gossip can be and still be so completely wrong. Pregnancy was the reason for the haste of our wedding, but not because I ever cheated. Chase laughed when he heard, saying everything worked out better than he hoped.

Only two people ever guessed at the truth.

Dad just came right out and asked. He and I were alone, and he was holding Abby for the first time. He stared at her for an eternity before asking me if she was Gabe's child. I'd never lied to him before, but I promised Chase no one would ever know she wasn't his, and that included my father. I hated the look of disappointment and defeat that came over him. Gabe left town a few days later, never knowing he fathered a child.

Brandi was the other, and I still didn't understand how she knew. When I talked to Chase about it, he told me to ignore her. He told me Brandi was a prostitute working in a strip club on the highway. I ran into her at the medical plaza after taking Abby for her three-month checkup. Trapped in the elevator with her as we descended to the street level, I tried to ignore her presence as she stared smugly at me from across the small space.

"Well, if it isn't Mrs. Carter and her little heiress to the kingdom," she sneered. "Chase is an idiot if he thinks anyone getting a good look at your brat isn't going to put two and two together." She tsked and shrugged her shoulders as the doors opened. "I can't believe everything he did just to marry you. Thanks for fucking up my life. I hope you have a nice life, bitch." She walked away leaving me gaping in confusion at her words.

Sometimes when I looked at Abby, I could see Gabe staring back at me. She was so beautiful. She had Gabe's dark brown eyes, except hers had flecks of green in them. Her hair was the same rich black color like patent leather, so shiny and curly. She had my nose and Gabe's chin, and she was just as stubborn and temperamental. She had no problem letting the world know when she was unhappy or wanted her daddy.

She was such a bundle of energy and spoiled rotten. Chase doted on her and even at almost four months, she had her daddy wrapped around her finger. He promised to love my child as his own, and he's kept that promise in spades. We decorated her room in shades of pink with a castle and magical forest painted on the walls. He even drew up plans to build her a castle playhouse in the yard this spring.

I was sad Chase's father never met her. He suffered another stroke midway through my pregnancy and passed away. The loss devastated Chase. It made me more determined to keep trying with my own father. Dad didn't agree with my decisions and disliked my husband, but he loved his granddaughter. He was almost as bad as Chase at spoiling her.

"I like the view, Mrs. Carter," he whispered.

I glanced down at the sheer black gown I wore, knowing it left nothing to the imagination. "I'm glad, since I bought it with you in mind. Did she wake up?" I asked. I walked over to stand beside them and stroked Abby's head before leaning down to meet Chase's lips in a soft kiss.

When we parted, he looked at her sleeping form in his arms and pressed another kiss to her forehead. "No, I just needed to hold her," he said quietly.

"I'm sorry Heather upset you tonight," I murmured. "You know I love you, right?"

He stood and carefully put Abby back in her crib, stroking her head to settle her back down. He turned to me and drew me to his side; leading me out of her room and down the hall.

"Chase?"

"Shhh. Don't talk."

He swung me up into his arms and strode to the bed. I wrapped my arms around his neck as his lips found mine. Our kiss became a firestorm of need as our tongues battled for dominance. He lowered my legs to the bed. Kneeling in front of him, I quickly unbuttoned his shirt as he yanked it from his jeans. I smoothed my hands over the firm planes of his bare chest. I leaned in to lick one of his nipples, smiling when he hissed. I kissed and nipped at his chest as he unbuckled his belt and quickly unbuttoned his jeans. My hands worked to release him as he discarded the last of his clothing.

He pushed me back on the bed and blanketed me with his body. I whimpered in need as he pulled at the straps of my gown, trapping my arms in their confines. He latched on to my breast and suckled deeply.

"Please," I moaned.

I felt the slide of material rising up my leg and the soft scratch of his fingernails. His fingers dove to the place I needed him the most and caressed me relentlessly.

"Chase!" I cried out, trying to raise my hips, anything to get closer.

He chuckled deeply at the sound of my mewling as I thrashed beneath him.

"That's right. Me. No one else. Ever," he growled possessively. He slid lower until his mouth took over where his fingers had been, sending me to such heights, I thought I'd go insane. With one hand, his fingers delved into my depths, driving me higher. His other kept me pinned to the bed. "You're mine, Karsyn."

"Yours. Only yours. Please, Chase, I need..." I cried. I was so close; I would say or do anything he asked in order to reach that peak I knew he would bring me to.

He pushed my gown up and over my head, throwing it on the floor as he covered me again before driving into me. I screamed at the sensation. He pulled my legs up to rest on his shoulders as he pounded into me over and over again. He brought me to an earth-shattering climax, and still he persisted. I stared into his glowing eyes as he thrust into me, seeking his own release. I felt just a flicker of fear at the intensity in his eyes. Emotions of love, possessiveness and fury flashed in his eyes.

I reached up to caress his face, understanding what he was feeling. Heather's comment about Gabe had upset him. I needed to bring him back from whatever precipice he was on. I loved Chase, but my love for Gabe remained, still claiming a part of me. Chase knew he battled for dominance in my heart though I'd never given him any reason to doubt my sincerity. I would always be his wife, and I loved him for everything he'd given me: love, security, a father for Abby. He deserved so much more love than I gave him.

"I love you, Chase. I love you. I love you," I whispered repeatedly until my words sank in. He pulsed inside me once more. Finding the release, he craved. He let my legs drop onto the bed while he stayed nestled between. His breath came in ragged shudders against my neck as I stroked his head.

He finally rose up to stare at me, brushing my sweat-matted hair away from my face. "I'm sorry, love. That's not quite what I had planned for tonight. Did I hurt you?" he asked worriedly.

I smiled and stroked his face. "That was certainly different, but no, you didn't hurt me. And you didn't hear me complaining, either."

He rolled to his back and brought me with him until I lay on top of him. We were quiet as he stroked my hair, and I listened to the beat of his heart. My eyes began to drift shut as I succumbed to sleep when he finally spoke.

"I love you, Karsyn. Everything I do is for you."

Chapter Twelve

January 26, 2009

Chase had been moody and irritable for weeks. Right after our anniversary, he decided on the spur of the moment to have an exterminator come spray the house for bugs. I told Chase I hadn't seen any, and it wasn't necessary. Chase snapped at me that it was his job to protect his family. He quickly apologized for taking his bad mood out on me and asked me not to tattle on him to Heather or my dad. I laughed at the sheepish look on his face and assured him his little temper tantrum would be our secret. When the exterminator came, Chase offered to take Abby to the office for the day while I spent a few hours getting pampered at the day spa near his office. I was relieved. I couldn't smell the chemicals when we got home that evening; however, Chase was livid at the report the exterminator gave him. He spent an hour yelling in his office at the poor guy about whatever he'd found.

When I asked what was wrong, he just said termites and not to worry. His constant brooding ceased when Abby and I came down with a stomach virus going around. He stayed home, taking care of us until he caught the bug too. I discovered Chase was a big baby when he was sick. He was as bad as Abby. I teased him about it, which seemed to help restore the peace in our home.

He apologized for being such a bear to live with. He assured me he was just upset over a business venture that went sour on him. He felt bad for working late and neglecting Abby and me. As an apology and surprise, Chase gave Heather and me a girl's weekend in New York to shop for our trip to Belize the following week. He arranged for Mrs. Murphy to stay at the house to help take care of Abby while we were gone. Chase said he was looking forward to some father-daughter time as well.

I was nervous about leaving Abby for the weekend but really excited about the trip. Heather and I hadn't had a weekend for girl time since high school. Heather was bummed we wouldn't be able to take the private jet again since it was being serviced for our trip next week. Instead, we would be flying first class—still pretty sweet.

I stopped at Heather's to pick her up on the way to the airport only to find out she caught the same stomach bug. She was as disappointed as I was about cancelling our trip. I left Heather in Justin's capable hands. He was working from home today and promised to take good care of Heather.

I left their house, contemplating going home or running a few errands. I called Mrs. Murphy to let her know she wouldn't need to stay all weekend after all. She suggested I go on my trip anyway and enjoy myself since she was there already. As I hung up, I thought about being in New York by myself. Without someone to share the sights or to go to dinner with, it would actually be a very lonely weekend, unless…

I turned my car around and drove back to the house. I quickly threw together a weekend bag for Chase and asked Mrs. Murphy not to say anything if he called. I kissed and hugged Abby again and left. I called the airline and booked us a later flight. I was going to kidnap my husband and take him to New York with me. It would be another way I could show my love for him. Since our anniversary, I felt like I needed to show my commitment and love even more. He tried to hide it, but he'd been on edge since that night. Something was bothering him, and I was going to do whatever it took to make my husband understand that I loved him.

I drove back to Chase's office in the city. Parking around the corner, I didn't want the garage attendant in Chase's building to ruin my surprise by telling him I was there. I glanced at my watch—almost noon. I figured we could grab a quick lunch before heading to the airport.

I worked against the stream of people coming out of the building for lunch and jumped into an elevator just as the door closed. I pushed the button to the eleventh floor and smiled to myself as I visualized the surprise in Chase's eyes when I told him I was kidnapping him. We're going to have so much fun even if we never left the hotel room.

The elevator doors opened, and I walked to the glass double doors marked Carter Enterprises, Inc. I saw the receptionist leading two very large men down the hall. I only caught a glimpse of them, but they seemed familiar. They both had black hair and were Hispanic. I puzzled over where I may have seen them when she came back to the reception area. I struggled to remember her name. She was the daughter of one of Chase's friends and was new with the company. I had only met her once before.

Her phone rang, so I waited while she answered the call.

"Good afternoon, Carter Enterprises. How may I direct your call?" She paused, listening to the person on the line, nodding her head. "Yes, Mr. Mendoza. Mr. Carter and his associates are already in conference, waiting for your call. Please hold while I transfer you to them." She punched a couple of buttons on the phone and waited. "Mr. Carter? I have Mr. Mendoza on the line for you." She looked up at me, and I quickly shook my head and put my finger to my lips. "If you don't need me, I'm going to leave for the day. Thank you, sir." She hung up and turned her attention to me.

"Hi, Mrs. Carter. I didn't expect to see you today. Aren't you supposed to be going to New York?" she asked curiously.

"Hi," I replied. I still couldn't remember her name. I winked and smiled at her. "I am, but I decided to steal my husband and take him with me."

She giggled and leaned in to whisper conspiratorially. "Well, I shouldn't be telling you this, but he's in a conference down the hall with the Belize office. The call I just put through is what they were waiting on. I don't think the meeting will take too long. His office is empty if you want to wait for him. And I happen to know he was planning on going home for the rest of the day after his meeting, so he's all yours."

I squeezed her hand and smiled. "Thank you so much."

She left, and I slipped into Chase's office, closing the door behind me. I sat in his chair and grinned at the pictures on his desk. Our wedding photo stood on the corner along with one of the three of us when Abby was born. The same picture was in the locket around my neck along with the picture of my parents. I sat for a few minutes then decided to use his private bath while I waited. I called the house to check on Abby again, and I heard my phone beep. I glanced at the screen, and the battery symbol flashed red.

"Damn phone," I grumbled.

I turned it off to save the last of my battery until I could put it on the charger and dropped the phone back in my purse. I made a mental note to tell Chase that I either needed a new battery or a new phone.

I'd just put my hand on the doorknob when I heard Chase's voice yelling at someone. I didn't want to interrupt so decided to wait. What shocked me was his language. In the entire time I had known Chase, I had never heard him like this. His voice was so cold, so full of anger.

He was furious. I felt a chill run down my spine as goose bumps broke out on my arms. I was actually afraid of him in that moment.

"Fucking hell! What do you mean she was at the house? She and Karsyn are supposed to be in the fucking air on their way to New York! I called Mrs. Murphy this morning and she told me Karsyn left the house in plenty of time, and I checked the airline schedule, and the flight left on time!" he yelled. "You better start explaining right now or so help me; your own mother won't recognize you when I'm finished."

"I don't know what to tell you, Mr. Carter," a man's voice responded. I could tell he was trying to placate Chase. Whatever he had to tell him, Chase was not pleased. "You said he'd be alone. We got in through the kitchen door, just like you said we would. He was walking down the hall when we popped him. He never saw us coming and went down without a fuss. The girlfriend came out of the bathroom and caught us. We had no choice but to pop her, too. We removed all of his equipment and papers we could find. The next shipment should still be safe."

"What's the big deal? So we popped the slut. Consider her a freebie," a second person said casually.

My head spun, trying to make sense of what I heard. Maybe I misunderstood. That's it, I didn't hear them right! I shook my head. It sounded too much like something from a James Bond movie or the Godfather. I thought about the voices. I knew them. A memory teased at the back of my mind.

"You want me to consider my wife's best friend a freebie? Are you shitting me? That's why I put her on a damn plane! If I wanted her dead, I would have told you! She isn't involved. She was too stupid to realize she was being used. She was actually a valuable source of information. Without her big mouth running off all the time, I wouldn't have suspected Justin Walker was DEA. She's the one who clued me in that Brandi was ratting us out to his fucking partner! She's the slut I want dead, not my wife's best friend! Do you have any idea what this is going to do to my wife?"

I heard shuffling, then the dial tone of his speakerphone. My voice came on telling the caller that I was unavailable and to leave a message. Hearing my voice on the phone brought me back to reality. My best friend was dead? Heather? A searing pain rushed through my chest, and I stifled a gasp.

"Karsyn, love, please call me the minute you get this message. It's extremely important. I need to know where you are and what happened to your flight this morning. Is everything alright? Call me ASAP, please. I love you," he said in the gentle, loving voice of my husband. The voice I heard every day of our marriage.

He disconnected the call and growled. I backed away from the door, staring at it in horror. I shook my head in denial. I clamped my hands tightly to my mouth to stifle the scream trying to break free.

I was trapped in this small room, forced to listen to my world fall apart. How did I not know I was married to the vilest of monsters? My husband was a murderer. Heather couldn't be dead. Justin couldn't be dead. I saw both of them only a couple of hours ago. No! Abby's Godmother, my best friend was not dead. I wouldn't believe it. My husband didn't have anything to do with the monsters in his office. I refused to believe it. It wasn't true. Even as I denied it, I knew. All the accusations and innuendos were true.

"Where the hell is my wife!" he screamed in rage. I heard the phone and other items hit the floor. He apparently shoved everything off his desk in anger.

"She may already know too much. Do you want us to eliminate her, too? This is why it's dangerous to marry outside of the business unless you're going to bring her into it," the second man said, his voice so cold and unfeeling. I could almost picture the uncaring shrug of his shoulders as he discussed the murder of two innocent people, offering to kill me, as well. I closed my eyes in fear of the answer my husband would give.

"You've made me break my promise to my wife twice, now," Chase said calmly.

I jumped when I heard the slide of a drawer open, followed by two quiet pops and the thud of something heavy hitting the floor. Bile rose in my throat as I realized what it was.

"Rot in hell, you son of a bitch. I still owed you that one for Karsyn's father. Fucking bastard was supposed to steal her passport and torch that shitty garage. Not put her father in the hospital. That little mistake cost me a fortune." He paused a moment before speaking calmly again. "Now, does that answer any questions regarding my wife? She is not to be touched. Not one hair on her head." There was a pause while he waited for the other person's response. "Now that we're clear, you have five minutes to tell me you've found that little bitch, Brandi, before I leave to find my wife."

I shuddered at the coldness in my husband's voice. He just killed a man in cold blood and continued his conversation as though nothing happened. I heard the creak of leather and the roll of the wheels of his chair as he evidently sat down. A throat cleared nervously.

"We can't find her. There isn't a single trace of her. That other agent vanished with her. Even our contact in the DEA doesn't know where they are. He isn't using the usual safe houses. Are you sure he pulled her in, and he isn't just holed up somewhere fucking her brains out? She is good at her job."

"No." Chase laughed darkly. "I would bet odds that agent," he spat, "wouldn't touch Brandi if you paid him money for the privilege. Hell, drugs couldn't get that bastard to give it up to her. Bitch still got the job done though. And I got Karsyn."

"So what do you want me to do now, Mr. Carter?" the voice asked nervously.

Chase growled in frustration. "Find the bitch!" he yelled, slamming his fists on his desk. "Find her and eliminate her! And I want it to hurt for what she said to my wife. Snoop around my father-in-law's place. I'm certain he's still in contact with that bastard. He's too sly to just roll over when I threatened to cut Karsyn and Abby out of his life completely. He won't risk losing them, but he hates me enough to keep trying."

I heard footsteps pause at the bathroom door and held my breath. I stared at the doorknob praying it wouldn't turn. He couldn't know I was here. Would he kill me if he found me?

"Call someone to come clean up this mess. Find Brandi and don't come back until you do. I've got to get the boys going on the search for my wife. I need to be with her when she gets the news about Heather. She's going to be devastated," he sighed. "God, this is not how this was supposed to go down. I made a promise to my wife never to cause her any tears. I do not like breaking my promises."

I heard the footsteps leave the office and the door shut. I continued to stare at the door, my brain shutting down, unable to process everything I'd just heard. I took a step back only to bump into the wall. I shook my head to clear it and walked quickly to the door. I grabbed the doorknob and turned it noiselessly, peering out carefully. I stepped out of the room and froze. I could feel the bile in my throat and quickly clamped my hand over my mouth. I didn't have time to give in to the nausea rolling in my stomach.

I'd only seen two dead people in my life, and they both died quietly in their sleep, not violently as the man on the floor in front of me. Blood seeped from the hole in his chest; darkening his navy shirt, and there was another hole in his forehead. I couldn't look away as I stared at his dead eyes. I remembered him. He was at the party Chase's friends threw us on our honeymoon. He worked security for the growers' consortium. Luis was his name, which meant the man who left with Chase was his counterpart, Francisco. They always came to the house in Belize to discuss shipment details. He was the one I misunderstood that day.

The clock on the bookcase chimed the half hour, which reminded me of my current situation. Thirty minutes. That's all it took to destroy my world. I stepped around Luis' body and ran for the door. I checked to make sure no one was in the hall or lobby and ran to the elevators. I got in and pushed the button to the first floor.

I leaned against the back wall and watched the numbers of the floors light up as the elevator descended. Tears trickled unchecked down my face. It was a losing battle; there would always be more.

The doors finally opened, and I stepped out, walking as calmly as I could to the entrance. Just as I entered the revolving door, I heard my name. I turned quickly in fear, my eyes landing on the security guard manning the front desk. He smiled and waved as I left the lobby, and I smiled weakly in return.

I walked hurriedly down the sidewalk in front of the building, my only thought was to get Abby and go to my dad's house. I glanced back through the glass wall at the security guard and noticed him on the phone. He seemed to be searching for someone. When his eyes connected with mine, I knew who he was looking for. He quickly said something and hung up the phone, running for the door.

I took off running down the sidewalk and crossed the street. I jumped into a parked taxi that was letting out the current passenger.

"Please, just start driving. I'll figure out where I want you to take me in a minute," I cried.

"Alright, Miss. Try to calm down and breathe," the driver said calmly.

He pulled away from the curb, and I turned back to see the security guard yelling at the garage attendant and sighed in relief. My brain was in overdrive, trying to figure out what to do. I needed to get Abby. I needed to tell my dad. I needed to call the police. I pulled my phone out and turned it back on. There wasn't much battery left, so I had to make the call count. I remembered Chase's instructions to Francisco. He was going to my dad's. I punched the speed dial on my phone and prayed he would answer.

Chapter Thirteen

I sighed in relief when my dad's voice came on the line.

"Hi Kari. Are you already in New York?"

"Daddy," I sobbed. "He-he killed them. They're dead. I'm scared. I don't know what to do. My whole marriage is a lie."

The rush of my father's breath was the only thing that told me he was still on the line.

"Kari, calm down. Tell me what's happened. Where are you? Is Heather with you? Where is Abby?"

I screamed in frustration as my phone beeped, reminding me that I had a limited amount of time. "Daddy, my phone is about to die. You have to leave. You aren't safe. Chase is sending someone to your house, now. He thinks you're working with agents or something. He had Luis and Francisco kill Heather and Justin. He killed Luis in his office. I heard everything." I paused to catch my breath, and a broken sob escaped my lips. "I'm so sorry, Daddy. I should have listened to you."

"Kari, where are you right now?" he demanded. I vaguely registered my father's lack of surprise at the accusations I'd leveled against my husband. Did he know all along that Chase was a criminal? Did he know the extent Chase would go to? Is that why he fought so hard to keep me away from him? I began to look at my dad's behavior in a new light. I caught the cab driver's gaze in the rearview mirror. He heard everything. I prayed I could trust him. I didn't have a choice if I was going to save my father and myself.

"I'm in a cab. I'm safe for now. You need to leave, though, before they get there. Please, Daddy," I cried.

"I'm leaving now, Kari," he assured me. "Where are you? Where's Abby?"

I was relieved when I heard the sound of his truck starting. My dad was safe for now. Now I just had to get to Abby. I knew instinctively Chase wouldn't hurt her, but I couldn't stand the idea of him being anywhere near her.

"Abby's at home with Mrs. Murphy; she's okay. Please just get somewhere safe, Daddy," I begged. "I can't lose you, too."

"You won't lo—" His voice cut out.

"Daddy? Daddy?" I yelled into the phone.

"Kari? I'm here. I'm calling Gabe. Where are—"

"Daddy?"

I looked at the black screen on my dead phone and threw it on the seat in frustration. I stared out the window at the passing buildings, trying in vain to put two thoughts together to figure out what to do. I had to get to Abby. My heart squeezed painfully at the thought of the danger. I had to get to my baby and keep her safe from Chase. I knew the cabbie wouldn't drive the hour it would take to get to the ranch to get her, but I didn't know if it was safe to go back for my car yet. I also didn't know where my dad was planning on going, and I couldn't call him to find out. What did that leave me?

I still couldn't face the fact that Heather was gone. My throat tightened, and I felt tears threatening to overwhelm me. We would never have the chance to laugh and gossip together. I lost the one person who knew my heart's secrets. I thought about her parents, who didn't know their only child was gone. I needed to get my daughter and get somewhere safe, and then I could mourn for my best friend.

"Ma'am, not that I mind, but do you know where you want to go yet?" the driver said, interrupting my thoughts.

I blinked and focused on where we were; we had literally been driving in circles. I looked down the side street as we passed Chase's offices again. My husband was standing on the corner giving orders to several men. I froze as he turned his head, and I saw complete fury in his expression. I pressed back into the seat and prayed he wouldn't see me as we drove past.

"Ma'am if you're scared of someone, I can take you to the police. It's just a suggestion," the driver offered courteously.

I nodded my head. "Please. I can't go back to my car, and I have to get my daughter."

He turned down a different street, opposite of the circle we'd been driving. After a couple of more turns, he stopped in front of the police department. I dug in my purse for my wallet to pay him.

"Don't worry about it, ma'am. You just get you and your daughter out of whatever trouble you're in." He smiled at me reassuringly as I squeezed his hand.

"Thank you for being so kind to me today," I said quietly as I got out.

"No problem, ma'am. You take care of yourself."

I watched him drive away before heading into the station. I bumped into a man who was leaving. I glanced up at him and apologized, continuing to the front desk. I almost missed the quizzical look he gave me as I passed.

"Can I help you?" the desk officer asked.

"I need to report a murder. Who do I talk to for that?"

I knew the only way to ensure the safety of my father and my daughter was for Chase to be in jail. I wanted him punished for hurting my father and killing Heather and Justin.

"Did you witness this murder, Miss...?" he paused, waiting for me to fill in the blanks.

"Carter. Karsyn Carter. Please, I need to get to my daughter. Is there someone I can talk to? My husband can't find me," I pleaded.

"I'll take over here," a deep voice interrupted.

I turned quickly to see the man I bumped into, standing behind me now. He looked down at me and smiled kindly.

"I'm Detective Mitch Davis. If you'll come with me, I'll take your statement." He gestured for me to precede him to a nearby elevator.

"Thank you. I need to get my daughter somewhere safe. Do you think an officer could take me to my house soon?"

"We need to get some details from you, and then I promise we'll take care of you, Mrs. Carter."

He led me from the elevator and down a corridor, passed a large office with several desks and officers at various tasks. He opened a door to a small room with a table and two chairs, holding out one for me to sit and taking the other for himself. He put a small tape recorder on the table and pressed the record button.

"Now, Mrs. Carter, please tell me who was murdered and what you know."

I proceeded to tell him everything I knew, breaking down partway through. Today I lost so much more than Heather. I lost the love and security I thought I had with Chase. My life was in shambles, built on a foundation of lies.

"Is that everything, Mrs. Carter?" he asked when I finally finished.

I thought about everything I said and the conversation I overhead. "Oh, something about next week's shipment being safe, but I don't know what the shipment is. That's everything I know."

He turned off the tape recorder and took out the miniature tape, putting it in his shirt pocket, then pulled out another and put it in the recorder. He smiled at my confusion.

"In case you think of anything else," he explained quickly. He stood and walked to the door.

"Please wait here, Mrs. Carter. I'm going to send someone to your friend's house to check it out. I'll be back in a few minutes."

"Thank you, Detective Davis. I need someone to take me home so I can get my daughter, and I would like to call my dad."

"Not a problem. I'll be back soon."

After he left, I stood and paced the room, unable to sit still. I recalled everything I thought I knew of my husband, finally seeing the lies for what they were. The tears gathered again as I closed my eyes in shame for being so naïve and stupid. I swallowed every single lie he ever told me. I took his side against my father, who was always there for me. I didn't deserve Gabe's love either. Even Gabe knew Chase wasn't to be trusted from the very beginning, and yet, I continually turned a blind eye. I never gave him my trust, always believing Chase over what was right in front of me.

My forehead fell against the wall as I remembered the last time I saw Gabe in my father's hospital room. There was a frantic edge to his voice as he tried to tell me, and I didn't listen. I thought about Abby and how this would affect her. She loved her daddy. No! I stopped myself. I raised my face to stare at the empty room and brushed harshly at my tears. Abby loves Chase, not her father, another sin to lie at my feet. My daughter had never met her father. I took her away from her him and gave her a monster in his place. I made a vow that when this was over, I would find a way to tell Gabe about Abby. I only hoped he would believe me and could forgive me in time.

I huffed as I looked at my watch. The detective left over an hour ago. I needed to get to Abby. I figured Chase would still be out looking for me so it would be safe to get her, but I was running out of time. I started for the door, determined to find someone to take me home. I stopped when I heard the lock turn and the door start to open. Why was it locked in the first place? I wasn't a criminal.

Detective Davis came in, and I quickly backed up, hitting the far wall with a whimper when I saw who followed him. My eyes darted from the entourage back to the detective.

"Why?" I whimpered.

His expression flashed guilt for only a moment before turning cold. He moved to stand off to the side, observing the scene that played out in front of him with boredom.

I turned to the men who filed into the room behind him. One was large and muscular and reminded me of a bouncer or bodyguard in his jeans, black t-shirt, and boots. Despite his size and menacing stance, he wasn't who caused my fear. The second man was Dr. Jensen, the doctor Chase insisted I switch to during my pregnancy. He was a friend of Chase's family, so would be certain to go along with Chase's deception. He ignored me while he pulled a syringe out of his jacket and filled it with fluid from a vial.

Even as my brain processed this information, my gaze stayed focused on the last man now closing the door behind him as he stared at me intently. I fought the hysterical laughter, which bubbled up at the concern in his eyes. I shook my head from side to side and choked back the sobs coming from deep within me.

Chase quickly strode forward and pulled me into his embrace; arms, which just last night, held me gently as we made love. "Karsyn, love, do you have any idea how worried I've been? I heard what happened to Justin and Heather. I can't believe they were victims of a home invasion. It's so sad. I'm going to miss them. You must be so distraught."

I tried to wrench myself free, and he only tightened his hold on me. "How could you?" I screeched. "You kil—"

I whimpered as I felt a sting on my arm and turned to see Dr. Jensen pulling away from me with an empty syringe. I looked up at Chase in fear. He smiled down at me and brushed my hair back, kissing my brow.

"It's just something to help you relax until I can get you home. You've had an extremely stressful day. I'm going to take good care of you, love. Don't worry." He turned to the detective. "Come by my office tomorrow, Mitch. There will be a nice bonus waiting for you at the front desk. Now I need to get my wife home. Thank you again for your help today."

He picked me up as I succumbed to whatever drug the doctor gave me. My eyes fluttered closed, and I felt his lips press against my head.

"That's right, love. Just rest."

Chapter Fourteen

May 1, 2009

I tucked Abby into the makeshift sling I'd made from the blanket in her diaper bag and pushed against the window, praying it wouldn't make too much noise. I shook my head against the fuzziness in my brain. I had to keep a clear head if we were going to get away. The guard standing outside the ladies' room wouldn't wait forever. I stood on the back of the toilet and dropped her bag out the window. I wrapped my arm securely around Abby as I swung my leg over the sill and carefully climbed out. It was just a short drop to the ground. I picked up her bag, ran to the corner, and walked quickly down the street.

Abby began to fuss and squirm in the sling.

"I know, baby. I'll get you something soon," I promised, kissing her head.

I looked behind me to be sure we weren't followed. I saw a taxi parked up ahead and held Abby tighter as I ran to it and climbed in.

"The bus station please," I said, as the driver pulled away from the curb.

I sank back into the seat in relief and untied the sling, settling Abby in my lap as I pulled a bottle out of her bag and fed her. I squeezed my eyes shut before opening them again, trying to fight against the familiar fog. I watched her drink her bottle and made faces at her to make her laugh. I looked out the back window several times to be sure no one was following us. I didn't want to think about Chase's reaction when he found out we'd escaped, much less what he'd do to me if he caught us.

"We're going on a little trip to visit Papa. Would you like that?" I said wistfully. "Maybe we'll even find your daddy. I'm so sorry Abby for taking you away from him. He is such a wonderful man, and you look so much like him. I hope one day he'll forgive me."

She stared up at me with Gabe's dark eyes, seeming to understand everything I was saying. I leaned down and kissed her soft head, holding her a little tighter.

The taxi came to a stop at the bus station. I gathered our things and paid the driver before heading to the ticket counter. I stared at the schedule on the wall, trying to make sense of what I was reading. The drugs Chase kept me on made it hard to think clearly. I finally gave up and told the clerk to give me two one-way tickets to whatever destination was loading next.

We settled into our seats on the bus. I drank the coffee I purchased from the small food court at the station, hoping the caffeine would help clear my head. I leaned back and closed my eyes. I had to find my dad. I didn't know where he was; only that Chase hadn't found him, so he had to be safe somewhere. I haven't seen or heard from him since that horrible day.

Today was only the third time Chase has let me out of the house after taking me home from the police station. He was testing how much control he had over me with the medication Dr. Jensen prescribed for my anxiety. My brain stayed in a fog so much of the time. I didn't even know what day it was anymore.

The first time had been for Heather's funeral. I stood beside the man who murdered my best friend and stared unblinking at the pink roses covering her coffin. I was so heavily drugged; I could barely walk and was unable to voice my condolences to her parents. Chase explained to them that I hadn't been well and was overwrought. He expressed our sorrow for her death.

He spent the first few days trying to get me to understand the reasons behind his actions. He loved me, and everything he did was for Abby and me. For all his crimes, he had only two regrets, Heather's death and my father's injuries.

He explained that he told my father of his intentions to marry me long ago. When my father forbade it, Chase threatened to destroy his business by pulling the contract and threatening anyone who used his garage. My dad seemed to give in by saying he'd agree if I loved him.

He sent Luis and Francisco to my dad's house on the morning of our wedding. The garage was punishment for bringing Gabe into my life. My father wasn't supposed to be there. He caught Luis in the act of setting the fire and confronted him. Luis took things too far. Chase assured me he never authorized my father's beating that landed him in the hospital, because to do so would hurt me.

He apologized for Heather, saying only Justin was supposed to die. Justin worked with Gabe and picked up where Gabe left off. He said the car accident that brought Justin into Heather's life was a setup. His only purpose was to find a way into Chase's confidence. He almost succeeded. Heather was an unfortunate incident. He pointed out, that he did try and get her out of town before it happened. If I'd only called him to tell him our trip was cancelled because of her illness, he would have had the hit carried out later. He told me everything boiled down to letting Gabe into my life.

He was right. Everything came down to my fault, my choices, and my poor decisions. Everyone I loved was hurt or dead because of me. The guilt buriedme. I truly had no one left to depend on but Chase, and I didn't want him. No excuse, no justification could undo the damage he caused.

When I told him I was leaving and taking Abby with me, he laughed and ushered in Dr. Jensen to shoot me up with whatever drug he gave me at the police station. The injections kept me in a fog until the pills I swallowed twice a day took over. Each time I got sick from the side effects, Chase was right there, holding my hair, cleaning me up, and telling me how much he loved me and hated doing this to me. He tried to assure me the medicine wasn't forever. It was only until I forgave him and was willing to forget the past.

The second time he let me leave the house was to determine if the pills gave him enough control over me in public. We went to the Double S for dinner. I sat wedged in the booth with Chase's arm firmly around my shoulders. Several of his men sat at tables or booths around us so no one could get close enough to question my behavior or for me to ask for help. I was so drugged; I couldn't have escaped or caused a commotion if the building was on fire. I don't even know if I ate the food in front of me or just stared at it all night.

Most people looked the other way, not wanting to become involved. Those in town who knew Chase were either working with him or afraid of him. Chase even had our police department firmly tucked in his pocket. My father, as far as I could tell, was the only one to ever stand up to him, and that was only because of me. Before, he was just as guilty of burying his head in the sand as the rest of us.

Tonight I took a huge risk. I didn't know if I could pull it off in my current mental state. I heard Chase talking on the phone to Francisco about needing to meet with a new associate but didn't want to leave me alone. He talked openly around me now. No need for secrets when your wife knew you're a murderer. The sugar investment wasn't sugar at all. It was cocaine. I began pouting that we never went out as a family anymore, and I wanted to go to one of our favorite Chinese restaurants in the city. He pointed out we had just been to the Double S a few days before, so I started crying. Tears came so easy these days, between the guilt and the effects of the medication. I told him I couldn't remember, and I felt like I was losing my mind. I was so inconsolable, he finally gave in.

He had several of his men with us just in case. I told him I needed to take Abby to the ladies' room to change her diaper. I remembered the window in the bathroom. He let me go while someone guarded the door. I still couldn't believe my plan worked and thanked God for watching over fools and children. I knew which category I fell into as I looked down at Abby now curled up and sleeping in my lap.

I inventoried what I had with us, and what I needed to do first when the bus stopped. I only had the two thousand dollars I'd stolen from Chase's dresser, a few diapers and a single change of clothes for Abby. I would need to find a hotel and a phone, get Abby food and diapers, and something more comfortable to wear besides my dress and heels. I hoped when I called my dad, he would have some idea how to keep Abby and I safe from Chase.

㈲ ⁊

I dropped the bags on the bed as I surveyed the dingy little motel room. We were in Talladega, Alabama outside of Birmingham; evidently, the destination I purchased. I put Abby down on a blanket on the floor with a couple of toys to keep her occupied while I put the milk and juice in the mini fridge. I left the rest of the food in the bag on the dresser. I dug out the change of clothes and a cheap backpack I purchased before finally sitting down. I grabbed my new prepaid cell phone and thanked God again for the kind saleslady who'd programmed the phone and explained how to pay for additional minutes when I needed. I took two aspirin, which would hopefully help with my never-ending headache, dialed my dad's cell phone number, and waited for the call to connect. I cried in frustration when the call went to his voicemail.

"Daddy? It's me. Please call me when you get this message. Abby and I are at a motel in Talladega, Alabama. I got away from Chase, but

I don't know where to go or what to do. I hope you're okay. I love you Daddy. I hope you can forgive me for everything. I bought a new cell phone so here's my number." I hung up and wiped the tears on my face.

Abby watched me from the floor where she played. I held my hands out and she crawled over for me to pick her up. I kissed her and rubbed noses to make her giggle. I hugged her close and rocked her for a few minutes.

"Mommy will give you a bath in a minute and then it's night-night time for you while Mommy tries to figure out what to do," I said wistfully.

She squirmed to get down, and I let her go play for a while longer. The cell phone rang shrilly in the quiet room, causing me to jump. I stared at it in fear for only a moment until I remembered the only person who had the number was my dad.

"Daddy?" I asked, timidly.

"Oh, Kari, thank God," his gushed in obvious relief. "I have been out of my mind worrying about you and Abby. No one could tell me anything. Heather's parents said you were at her funeral with Chase." His voice was laced with frustration and confusion now. "How could you do that? What could he possibly have said to convince you to stay with him after that? What's happened to you, Kari?"

I shut my eyes. Of course with my track record my dad would think that. The weight of my guilt and shame buried me. I wanted to pull the blankets over my head and never come out again. I wanted someone to hold me and tell me everything was going to be okay, but no one would let me forget that everything was my fault. My emotions were at war with each other. I was ashamed for my stupidity. I brought Chase into our lives and refused to see the destruction he caused to everyone. I was as guilty for the death of my best friend as if I pulled the trigger myself. I was guilty for my father's injuries. I was guilty of hiding

Abby from Gabe and not trusting him. I was guilty of so many crimes that the only thing I could do was lash out in defense.

"Daddy, Chase has been keeping me a prisoner," I cried. "This is the first chance I've had to leave him."

"Why didn't you go to the police, Kari?" he sighed.

"I did, Daddy! A dirty cop turned me right over to Chase! He keeps shoving pills down my throat which keep my head so fuzzy I don't know which end is up anymore." I felt the walls closing in around me as my heart started racing. My head was pounding and perspiration beaded on my scalp. My stomach began churning, and I knew I was about to get sick. "Daddy, I have to go. I don't feel so good. I think it's the pills. Please come get us. I love you." I gave him the address of the hotel, and he assured me he'd be here by morning.

I snapped the phone shut and threw myself on the bed sobbing. I pressed my hands against my temples tightly. I was an emotional wreck and stressed out. Coming down off the medication for the past two days wreaked havoc with my mind. The stabbing pain in my head only made things worse. I couldn't cope with anything anymore. I bathed Abby, and crawled in bed with her. Maybe things would be better in the morning.

Chapter Fifteen

I woke slowly. My head felt heavy, and my limbs felt like lead weights. My mouth was dry and had a funny taste. I groaned and turned my head from side to side trying to open my eyes. My stomach knotted in pain; I felt sick. I stumbled out of bed to run to the bathroom and froze.

I looked around the room; nothing was familiar. I had gone to sleep in a cheap dingy motel room and awoke in a large, luxurious bedroom with an iron king-size bed covered in rich bedding and a gauzy canopy hanging from the ceiling. French doors led to a balcony beyond with the same gauzy covering over the glass.

I rubbed my temples, trying to remember. I talked to dad on the phone. I gave Abby a bath, and then we went to sleep. I stopped immediately and swung back to the bed.

Abby!

Fear gripped me. Where was she? My stomach lurched again, and I quickly ran to the bathroom. After a few minutes, I stumbled out again. I looked down at my clothing. I no longer wore the cheap department store t-shirt and jeans from earlier. I now wore one of my nightgowns from home.

I sank down on the side of the bed with my shoulders slumped in defeat and started crying. Chase had found us; it was the only logical conclusion. I gave myself only a moment for tears. The time had come to face my husband and admit my failure. He would never give me the opportunity to escape again, and I knew it. I had my one shot at freedom and blew it. I wiped my eyes and brushed my hair back from my face. Squaring my shoulders to face my husband, I opened the door to see where I was.

I left the room and started down the hallway. I looked over the balcony to the large living room below and descended the stairs, listening for any sounds or voices that would tell me where to find Chase and Abby.

"Chase! Let's get this over with." I waited but got no response.

"Abby! Come to Momma, sweetheart!" I began to feel uneasy when I didn't hear Abby's usual squeals or the patter of her little hands and knees slapping against the floor as she crawled.

"Chester Wayne Carter stop fucking around, you prick!" I yelled again.

I smirked, listening to myself. It gave me a sense of bravado, which help to cover the fact I was scared of my sure-to-be-wrathful husband. I figured my outburst would gain an immediate response, if nothing else. Chase was always adamant I act like a lady, and ladies didn't curse. Still I waited. The silence was beginning to get to me.

I wandered the house while listening for any sign of Chase. Wherever he was, Abby had to be with him. I searched the bedroom, living room, and dining room. I found a small library full of books along with an office and another bedroom with a twin bed and crib set up; the pink bedding was still in its packaging. Another bath and laundry room finished my tour. I finally looked out the windows of the living room and noticed palms, ferns, white sand, and rocks. I wondered if we were in Belize.

I ran to the door but found it locked with an electronic keypad. My heart skipped a little in trepidation but refused to acknowledge it. Instead, I turned to go out the door I'd seen in the kitchen. It also had a keypad, and without the combination, I wouldn't be leaving through a door.

"Fine, you want to play games and be an ass, I'll just go out the fucking window," I told the empty house. I went back to the long windows in the living room and tried to open them. They wouldn't budge, and I couldn't find the locking mechanism.

"Alright, jackass, you just lost yourself a perfectly good fucking window. You're just going to have to deal with it," I told the air around me as I searched for something to throw. I settled on an ugly stone sculpture sitting on the coffee table and threw it at the glass. I yelped and jumped when it bounced off, not even leaving a scratch. What the hell? I stooped, picked it up, and walked up to the window again. This time I held onto it and again, tried to smash the glass. It didn't budge.

Panic hit me fully in my chest, and adrenaline pumped through my racing heart. I went from room to room, trying to break any window to no avail. I was trapped inside this house with no way out. I went back to the living room and listened again for any sounds of life. I could only hear the roar of blood rushing in my ears.

"You've made your point!" I stopped and waited. Nothing. "Chase! Please, you're scaring me now! Please come out!" Still silence. I slid down the wall to the floor, pulled my knees to my chest, and started sobbing. I leaned my head back against the wall and screamed with everything I had in me. "Chase!"

I was going into hysterics and shaking. I began to wonder if he were leaving me here to die as punishment for running away. I crawled up onto the sofa and curled into the fetal position, holding a pillow. I cried for my dad, who I would never see again. I cried for my daughter. I would never see her grow into the beautiful young woman she was destined to be. She would have her sweet, innocent personality molded by Chase.

I awoke some time later to the sound of a phone ringing from somewhere in the house. I quickly got up and wiped my face, gulping air to calm down. I listened and heard the ring again. I sobbed in relief and ran to find it. It came from a phone I hadn't noticed in the office earlier. I snatched up the receiver.

"Chase, please let me out," I sobbed. "Where's Abby?"

"Karsyn, love, I hate to see you cry. I'm sorry I couldn't be with you when you woke, but it was unavoidable. Don't worry, though; I'll see you soon. How do you like your new home? Isn't it beautiful? You're going to be very happy once you've settled in. I know how much you love the ocean."

"Chase, please don't leave me here. I promise I won't ever run away again," I started sobbing. "Please, I need Abby."

"That's enough!" he snapped, anger creeping into his voice. He paused to take a breath and gain control again. "Now, I'm going to be there in time for dinner. Wear your hair down for me; you know how much I love your hair."

I closed my eyes, trying to silence my sobs. I nodded my head and whispered, "Please tell me where Abby is. Is she alright?"

"Abby is fine, love. She's back where she belongs. She was excited to see her daddy. That wasn't very nice of you to kidnap my daughter. You and I are going to have to discuss the ramifications of your recent actions. I was only just able to get you and Abby out of that motel ahead of that fucking agent and his little band of idiots," his said, his voice laced with the anger he kept in check. "If he had gotten to you first, Karsyn, their blood would be on your hands."

"My dad? Was he there?" I asked hesitantly. I closed my eyes and felt the moisture of tears as they ran down my face. I had been so close. If only I had called immediately from the store instead of waiting for the privacy of the hotel room.

He sighed. I wondered if he would answer me or not.

"Yes, Karsyn, he was there as well. I still haven't decided what I'm going to do about him. I know you talked to him, but he can't prove anything. It would hurt you if I eliminated him, so he's safe, for now."

His voice lowered to that seductive tone that used to make me tremble for him. My stomach twisted and my lip curled in disgust. "I can't wait to see you. You're so beautiful, but you need to get dressed and eat something."

My hand automatically clutched at my gown. I didn't understand how he knew. My eyes darted around the room and located the cameras in the upper corners of the room. My eyes widened in fear. He could see me.

"That's right, love. Blow me a kiss," he chuckled.

I continued to stare at the camera.

"Karsyn, I'm going to think you don't love me anymore," he warned darkly. "I'll be extremely disappointed if that's the case."

I raised shaky fingers to my lips and blew a kiss at the camera.

He laughed louder. "Soon, love, very soon.

Chapter Sixteen

September 5, 2009 (Present Day)

I opened my eyes and stared unseeing, for a moment, as I slowly came back to the present. I brushed absently at the wetness on my face as I held my locket as a talisman in my other hand. Tears were always there when I remembered. My first month on the island was agony, not that it was any less now. I just didn't make the same mistakes anymore; I couldn't live with the consequences.

In the beginning, I fought tooth and nail against my confinement. I couldn't smash the windows, but I could throw things, tear things, break things; and that first day I did. I also used a kitchen knife to cut my hair. The result was an extremely angry Chase calling to tell me to look out the window at the dock when he arrived. I saw his yacht anchored off shore and the smaller boat approaching. My heart sped up with anticipation when I saw Abby's dark curls blowing over Chase's shoulder.

I stood at that window, locked away, and watched him step off the boat with Abby in his arms. He tossed her up in the air, playing with her on the dock while my heart ached for my baby. He said something to her, pointed at the house, and helped her blow a kiss in my direction. He then turned and handed her to someone on the boat, and the dinghy pushed off, returning to the yacht, leaving only my malicious husband. My punishment lasted two months before I saw Abby again; until my hair began to grow back; until I was willing to talk and act like a lady, again; until I could treat him with the same love and respect as I did before.

He taunted me with news of how big Abby was getting, how she was learning to walk, how she was talking more, and how much she missed her mommy. He told me about the woman who was working in our home, helping to care for Abby in my absence. He laughed, thinking I might be jealous of another woman, assuring me he only had eyes for me. He could have a hundred women for all I cared. I only cared about Abby, and I hated that someone else was taking care of my daughter.

Chase visited me every weekend during that time. Why deny himself the pleasure of my company? This was my punishment, not his. I fought him every time he touched me. He would just hold me down, always whispering in my ear how much he loved me and how much Abby missed me. He constantly reminded me the choice was mine. He held me so tenderly the night I cried in defeat, finally giving up the fight. I wanted my daughter more than I hated him.

I sniffed and took a shuddering breath as I fought back a fresh wave of tears. Outside was the only place I was free to cry. Inside he monitored me, and crying meant I still had some fight left in me. I might be alone on this godforsaken island, but Chase controlled me as easily as if he were here. He kept me locked away in the house for the first two weeks until I learned to follow the rules. I have free run of the island but only at certain times of the day. Neglecting to come back inside so he could observe me would result in finding myself locked up again. The window and door locks could only be activated and deactivated by Chase. He would never give me the means to lock him out of his own home. The windows were bulletproof glass, which used to make me wonder who owned the island before Chase.

He laughingly told me how Gabe, along with several DEA agents, showed up at the ranch with a warrant. They searched for any evidence of my accusations, which would have tied Chase to Justin and Heather's murders. Abby was there with Chase and her new nanny. Everything was as it should be, except I wasn't there.

The story he circulated was that I had a nervous breakdown after Heather's death and my father's abandonment of me. Dr. Jensen confirmed I was in a private hospital in Europe undergoing treatment for severe depression and paranoia. He said I was prone to hysterics and hallucinations, and had to be hospitalized for my own safety. He had high hopes I would return home soon. Chase played the distraught husband so well; even the judge offered his sympathy. All charges against him were dropped for lack of evidence. Nothing ever touched him. I was the only witness to his crimes and confessions, and anyone looking for me was searching on the wrong side of the world. I was safely hidden away on a small private island off South America.

I turned toward the dock, and a smile spread across my face. I ran back inside and erased all evidence of my tears. I slipped on my sandals before running down the stairs. I sprinted down the beach and waited impatiently at the end of the dock. I saw her in Chase's arms squealing and giggling as he tickled her and played with her. I started laughing and waving, blowing kisses to her while I waited for the crew to tie off the dinghy.

She squirmed in his arms to get down when she finally noticed me, but he held her firmly until they were off the boat.

"Come on, Princess. Let's show Mommy how good you can walk now," he smiled.

"Hi, baby, I've missed you so much!" I cried. I started sobbing and laughing at the same time. "Oh, look how big you've grown!"

I knelt on the dock and held my arms out to her. She toddled into my embrace as soon as Chase put her down, and I swung her up, spinning her around. I rained kisses all over her face and hugged her tight. This was always so hard on me. The only thing harder was when she left.

"And where is my love, Karsyn? Aren't you happy to see me as well?" Chase asked as he walked up to us.

He took Abby from me and handed her to the older woman who'd just stepped off the boat. I hated having her here. She was nice to Abby but treated me with nothing but disdain. As far as she was concerned, I was too naive to be a proper wife in Chase's world. She thought he should have cut his losses and buried me, not set me up in an ivory tower.

"Mrs. Wilson, please take Abby up to the house and get her settled. My wife and I will be along in a minute."

I watched her take Abby down the dock toward the house and then turned to face my jailer.

"Hello, Chase, you're looking well," I said, fighting to keep the hatred from my voice.

I walked up to him and dutifully tilted my face up for his kiss. I hated him with every fiber of my being now, but for Abby, I would endure anything. If I wanted to spend time with Abby, I had to accept my husband's love. Chase brought her to visit me every other week. However, if I didn't show the proper amount of love toward my husband, he would send her back to the yacht.

He wrapped his arms around me and gave me a passionate kiss. In my other life, this would have taken my breath away and made my knees weak. Now it only repulsed me.

"You look beautiful, as always, love." He smiled as he took in my appearance, running his fingers through my hair. "It's growing back, finally. I'm pleased you're resting more. It's too hot for you to be outside in the middle of the day."

I clenched my teeth and gave him a tight smile. "If you'd let me come home, you wouldn't need to worry so much about me," I reminded him.

His eyes narrowed. He leaned down, and his lips trailed down the side of my neck, stopping to suck and bite on the flesh of my shoulder. He rose up just enough to kiss the mark I knew he'd left. I always carried his brand on my body as a reminder of him when he wasn't here.

He held my face in his hands and sighed. "Karsyn, this hurts me as much as it does you. I love you and nothing would make me happier than to have you home where you belong." His thumbs brushed against the slight puffiness still under my eyes. "You think I don't know you still cry. Maybe it was a mistake to bring Abby today."

My eyes filled with fresh tears and spilled at his threat. I clutched frantically at his shirt and raised myself on my toes trying to reach his lips. I wrapped my arms around his neck and pulled at him. Smiling, he tilted his head down and let me kiss him desperately. I needed him to feel my sincerity before he called for the boat and took Abby away from me again. I couldn't miss her first birthday.

"No! Please, don't. I miss Abby. I miss being with you. That's the only reason I'm crying, I promise. I hate that she's so far from me, and I don't get to be there to watch her grow. I want to come home and show you I can be a good wife again," I begged. "I know I was wrong to leave. I understand that you only did what you had to because you love me. I swear. I'm ready to come home. I promise I only want to make you happy. I want to be a family again. Please, I'll do anything, Chase. Please let me come home."

His hand moved from my face to settle on my stomach. His eyes grew darker, and his voice deepened. "I think it's time we had another baby. Abby needs siblings, and I want a son to carry on my name. Show me you're completely committed to our marriage. When you're pregnant with my child, I'll bring you home."

Chapter Seventeen

It has been three days since Chase and Abby left. I held onto the memories of that weekend. We built sand castles with her on the beach, blew bubbles, and watched her try to catch them in her small hands. We sang Happy Birthday to her and cheered with her as I helped her blow out the candle on top of her cake. But I felt complete when I rocked her to sleep at night, not wanting to let her out of my arms for even a moment.

Of course, with these came the unwelcome memories of Chase taking her from my arms and leaving her with the nanny before leading me to our bedroom and shutting the door. I would force myself to draw on whatever strength I had from deep within me to take the initiative by having sex, submitting to my own personal hell, showing him I was fully committed to our marriage, and giving him a baby.

My shoulders shook with racking sobs. Chase had me completely trapped. The only way to be with Abby was to give him a child, and the moment I become pregnant with Chase's baby, I would never escape. His plan to relocate to Belize ensured I had no one to turn to for help and no hope for escape. He was even more powerful there than at home. Everyone knew exactly who and what he was and strived to stay in his good graces. That meant keeping me completely under control. His ultimatum successfully destroyed any fight left in me.

I stood and brushed the sand off my shorts. I slowly walked back down the beach toward the house. Soon it would be time for Chase's afternoon call.

As I came around the bend, I was so wrapped up in my thoughts that I didn't notice the boat tied to the dock or the men armed with automatic weapons, swarming the island. I heard someone shout and looked up to see a man gesturing to me as he yelled to another man who was starting toward the house. My heart skipped in fear when he whipped around. Wearing a black baseball cap that obscured his face, he changed directions and sprinted in my direction while slinging his rifle over his shoulder. I didn't see Chase among them, but their weapons were enough for me to know it wasn't a social call.

My eyes darted to the house, and I debated the wisdom of trying to run to the house or back down the beach. Neither prospect held much hope against armed men, but in the house, I stood a chance, however small. I took off running and heard several shouts as they ran to intercept me. Someone grabbed me from behind and bodily lifted me from the ground. I screamed and clawed at the arm that held me, struggling to get away.

"Stop fighting, Karsyn. You're safe now."

I ceased struggling as his words sank in and turned to look into the eyes of the man I thought I'd never see again.

"Gabe? Are you really here?" I whispered in awe.

My hand trembled as I reached up to touch his face, wanting to assure myself he was real. I saw a flicker of emotion in his eyes before they became cold and distant again. He released me and took a step back, putting me out of reach.

"Mrs. Carter, you're a very hard person to track down. We have a warrant to take you in for questioning regarding your husband's involvement in the deaths of Agent Justin Walker and Heather Roberts, as well as, assault, extortion and drug trafficking. If you'll please come with us," he stated formally, gesturing toward the boat.

I looked at the boat and shook my head, turning back to him. "I can't," I said desperately. "You don't understand what he'll do if I leave." I couldn't face the thought of never seeing my daughter again. If I left, Chase would find me. He would take Abby away from me forever as punishment.

"Mrs. Carter, I'm afraid you don't have a choice in the matter," he said, anger burning in his eyes as he stared me down. "Aren't you interested in seeing Chase Carter brought to justice for the attack on your father or your best friend's murder? Do you love him so much you'd let him get away with everything he's done?"

I stared at him for a moment in disbelief before the anger bubbled up inside of me. Seven months of having to hide my feelings and keep it all buried suddenly found an outlet. I launched myself at him in rage, beating his chest and arms with my fists.

"How dare you! You can't begin to know what that bastard has put me through! I hope he rots in Hell! Don't you dare stand there and accuse me of not caring. I've lost everyone I love because of him! He's done nothing but manipulate me and play me for a fool. I hate him with everything I am, but I can't leave! Gabe, he has my baby. I'll never see her again if I leave," I sobbed brokenly as all the fight went out of me at the thought of how hopeless everything was.

He wrapped his arms around me and leaned down to growl in my ear. "I know that fucking bastard has my daughter, Karsyn. That bastard set me up, and you ran straight into his arms, taking my daughter with you. But don't worry; he won't have her for long. There's already a team in place to rescue Abby. I will get her back, and when I do, you and I are going to have a long overdue talk."

I stilled at his words, and I closed my eyes in dread. "How did you find out?"

He released me, and I stepped back to face him again. I still saw the justified anger in his eyes, but now I also saw the hurt my betrayal had caused. He stroked my cheek with the back of his hand as he stared at me thoughtfully.

"You didn't deny or defend yourself from the gossip that you slept with him while we were together. You even lied to your own father. I knew it wasn't true, but I let my anger and pride rule my decisions. I can only imagine what you must have been feeling that night, but how could you ever think I would betray you? I loved you, Karsyn." He cleared his throat and was all business again.

"You may have let everyone believe Abby was his, but blood doesn't lie. Abby's blood was typed when she had jaundice as an infant. Abby is AB negative. Chase is O positive. I know for a fact she isn't his. Now we need to leave before the boat that patrols the island makes another pass. Let's go."

Gabe grabbed my elbow and led me to the boat. Once on board, I stared at the water churning in the wake of the engine, trying not to feel the anger and hurt emanating from the man whose love I had kept locked away in the recesses of my heart for so long. My thoughts churned between Abby's safety, holding her in my arms again, seeing my dad again, and lastly, Gabe's words. He loved me. Past tense. No more. There was no way to apologize for taking the first year of Abby's life from him. I could only hope that somehow he would let me make amends and, at least, try to be friends for Abby's sake.

I turned from staring at the rushing water and let my gaze drift stopping briefly on each man in the boat with me. I took in their matching combat boots, fatigue pants, Kevlar vests, and black t-shirts emblazoned with DEA on the back. I let my gaze rest on Gabe's back, soaking in the sight of him even as he ignored me. My eyes narrowed angrily as I stared at the same DEA stamped on his back. He was an agent, as well. He wasn't a mechanic. I thought back over our fights regarding Chase and the conversation I overheard between him and my dad before Christmas. He never loved me. The son of a bitch used me for his own gain! He wasn't interested in being with me other than helping his own agenda! His only concern was bringing down Chase. He said when this was over we were going to talk...oh boy were we going to talk. I may have been nothing more than a convenient piece of ass for him, but we had a daughter. She was all that mattered to me now. He will need to decide if he wants to be a part of her life or not, and based on his explanations, I will need to decide if I'm going to let him near her.

Chapter Eighteen

I woke to the feel of someone stroking my hair. It took a moment for me to remember where I was. I was no longer on the island; Gabe rescued me. We flew on a military transport from an obscure location back to the States. I was now in a cabin hidden in the mountains of West Virginia. At least, I think that's what I was told. I was so exhausted, I was asleep before my head even hit the pillow.

I stared at the dark form sitting beside me on the bed. I knew who was with me.

"Hi," I whispered.

"I'm sorry. I didn't mean to wake you," he replied quietly.

I shifted under the blanket and moved to sit up. He pressed his hand against my shoulder stopping me.

"No. Go back to sleep. I need to leave anyway. I just wanted you to know I'm heading out to meet the teams that have your father and Abby. We should be back in a few days. I'm leaving Agent Johnson in charge in my absence. He'll take care of anything you need."

"Gabe-" I started.

"Shh. We'll talk when I get back, I promise. Not now. There isn't time, and we have a lot to talk about. Just sleep for now."

He leaned down and pressed his lips to mine in a gentle kiss reminiscent of the kind we use to share. He pulled away just as it became heated and swiftly left the room, closing the door quietly on his way out. My fingers ghosted over my lips still tingling from his kiss and I smiled before drifting back to sleep.

Ↄ ↄ

I paced the living room, impatiently listening for any sounds that would indicate their arrival. Gabe called yesterday, assured me they were on their way, and should arrive later today. I was driving the agents with me crazy. I'm sure I sounded as bad as a kid on a road trip. My constant "Any word yet?" was always followed by a clipped "No." Their answers had been nicer three hours ago.

I couldn't breathe until I held my baby in my arms again. My fear for her safety outweighed any feelings of apprehension about Chase finding me. Gabe had timed everything so Chase's attention would be divided. He would have to choose who was more important to him, Abby or me. Gabe gambled correctly that I was Chase's primary concern, allowing the other team to get Abby out of Texas safely. He said reports indicated Chase had left Texas and was on his way to South America.

The house I was in was only accessible by helicopter or the one rough and rocky, dirt road, which wound through the trees up the mountainside to the house. There was no way for Chase to find us. Even if he did, there were two men inside at all times and another two patrolled outside. We would finally be safe.

I heard the static of a radio in the next room and stopped pacing, holding my breath in anticipation. When Gabe's voice announced they were coming up the drive, I squealed and clapped my hands. I ran to the door only to slam into a wall of muscle—Agent Johnson. He was a huge man at least as tall as Gabe, but wider. He had salt and pepper hair and laughing blue eyes. The other agents jokingly called him Pops due to his age and demeanor. He took his job seriously and was by the book.

"Please get out of my way," I asked impatiently.

He smiled in understanding but shook his head at me.

"Sorry, Mrs. Carter, but you need to stay inside and away from the windows until we get the all clear. It'll only be a few more minutes," he assured me.

I stomped my foot in exasperation.

"I heard Gabe on the radio. He's coming up the drive," I groaned, pointing outside the window. "I want to see my daughter. Please? I need to see her. I promise to stay on the porch," I begged.

I stuck out my lower lip in a sad pout. It was worth a try and had always worked for me in the past. He just chuckled and shook his head again.

"I'm sorry, but I'm married and have two daughters and a granddaughter. That pout doesn't work on me. I'm immune," he laughed. "Stay inside, please."

With that, he walked outside and shut the door firmly behind him. I moved to the window only to see him standing on the other side, shaking his finger at me.

"Fine," I huffed.

I stuck out my tongue, earning another laugh before he walked off the porch, pulling his weapon from the shoulder harness as he went. I heard another deep chuckle coming from behind me and swung around to face Agent Adams. Besides Chase, he was by far the sleaziest man I had ever met. He was tall and thin, and kept his black hair slicked back. With his New Jersey accent and gold chain around his neck, he seemed more like a gangster than a federal agent. He considered himself a Casanova or something. If he didn't make me laugh so much, he'd make my skin crawl.

"What?" I snapped in irritation.

"Maybe if you ask me nicely, I'll let you go outside." He winked and turned his face to tap his finger against his cheek, indicating a kiss on the cheek would be my payment.

"Ugh! Does anyone actually fall for that?" I asked, disgusted and turned away to stare out the window.

He laughed loudly. "It's all about demographics, sweetie. Back home, I'm considered quite the catch. I guess my charm just doesn't work on small-town Southern girls. Y'all seem to prefer the sweet cowboys with the white hats and belt buckles the size of dinner plates." His exaggerated attempt at a Southern drawl was cringe worthy.

"Not all of us," I mumbled. No, this small-town girl stupidly preferred men who weren't who they claimed to be. Men who played me for a fool, made me love them, only to find out later it was all an illusion, a lie. And I had done it twice!

Gabriel Thompson was no mechanic. He was a federal agent who used me. I was nothing but a pawn in his quest to bring down Chase Carter's empire. I still didn't know anything about him other than that. There was no reason for anyone to share personal information about him with me. I was just a witness to bring their fellow agent's killer to justice. Where that left my daughter, I had no idea. She obviously hadn't been part of his plan.

My husband wasn't who he pretended to be either. He wasn't my personal Superman. He was a wolf in sheep's clothing, and I had willingly been lead to slaughter. I never questioned what was right in front of my face and swallowed all the crap that came out of his mouth. I married a man who gave drugs to children. I had seen more than one friend in school become hooked on drugs and spiral out of control.

And this was the man who my daughter called Daddy. I shuddered, suddenly cold. I rubbed the goose bumps on my arms. What was I going to do? What was going to happen to us now?

The sound of tires crunching on the gravel drive interrupted my depressing thoughts. I fought the urge to rush for the door as Agent Adams reminded me to wait. He pulled his gun and motioned for me to move to the corner of the room as he stationed himself by the window to watch. I strained to see what was happening from my position across the room. A flash of sunlight hit chrome as two large black SUV's stopped in front of the house. I waited for what seemed an eternity before a voice outside shouted, "All clear." The tension in Agent Adams shoulders disappeared, and he turned and flashed a smile at me as he put away his gun.

"Look who's here." He grinned as he opened the door.

I ran forward but then stopped, my hands rushing to my mouth to stifle my cry. My baby! Gabe strode down the hall with her in his arms; she was wrapped in a blanket.

"What happened to her?" I shrieked, racing after him.

He ignored me as he carried her to my room and laid her on the bed. He gently unwrapped the blanket from around her and smoothed her hair from her sleeping face. I rushed forward and scooped her up, cradling her in my arms. Quiet sobs escaped me as I held my baby girl.

"Abby, baby? It's Mommy. Please wake up," I cried, stroking her hair. I looked up at Gabe with tear-filled eyes. "What happened to her?"

He sat on the bed beside me and stroked her head. He seemed to be mesmerized by her. He smiled reassuringly to me.

"She's fine," he whispered. "We had to give her a very mild sedative for the trip. She should wake up soon."

"You drugged my daughter?" I hissed, hugging Abby closer to me. It seemed I could never protect her. "Do you not care at all? Not even Chase would ever think about drugging her."

His gaze snapped to mine as his hand stilled on her head. His eyes narrowed, and I saw the suppressed anger burning in their depths. He stared at me a moment before standing and stepping away from us with his fists clenched at his sides and a tic in his jaw. I held my breath, reminding myself that I didn't know this Gabe.

"She was scared being surrounded by strangers. She hasn't seen your father since she was four months old. She didn't know him either. I gave her something to help her sleep so she wouldn't be afraid," he said slowly. I could tell he was fighting his anger at my accusations. "Chase Carter wouldn't have to sedate her though, would he? She thinks he's her father. She knows him. She doesn't know me. Would you prefer she spent the last week being terrified and crying? Do. Not. Ever accuse me of not caring for my daughter."

Shame washed over me at my accusations. I hadn't thought about the fact she would be surrounded by strangers and afraid. Gabe had done what was necessary to protect her the only way he could.

"I'm so—" I began.

"I'm not interested in your apologies. Just save them. Tend to our daughter, and I'll send your father back to visit you."

He turned on his heel and quickly left the room.

I looked down at Abby and kissed the top of her head as I laid her back down on the bed. I shifted her to the center of the mattress and covered her again. I got up and tiptoed down the hall to find Gabe. I needed to apologize. It seemed that's all I ever did anymore. Maybe one day I'd quit making the same mistakes and do something right for a change. I stopped in the hallway when I heard voices coming from the living room.

"That's your little girl in there, isn't it?" Agent Johnson asked.

"Pops, don't start, now isn't the time. I need to get Mr. McKenna and take him to visit his daughter and granddaughter. Everything was in my report. I did what was necessary for the assignment. You know what it's like going undercover; whatever it takes to get the fucking job done," Gabe growled.

My breath hitched at his words, and I closed my eyes against the pain. I was only a job to him, nothing more. Tears slid down my cheeks. I thought the kiss he gave me before he left meant something, but evidently not. I turned to go back to my room in defeat when I heard Agent Johnson laugh.

"Everyone else may buy that tough guy act you put on, but you forget who you're talking to. Don't bullshit me, Agent Thompson. I've known you since you were a wet-behind-the-ears rookie trying to prove you could make it without your father's name behind you. That girl and your daughter are more than an assignment to you. I'm going to tell you something too; not agent to agent, but as your friend and mentor."

"Yeah, and what's that?" His voice sounded dejected and resigned.

"Pull your fucking head out of your ass and tell that girl the truth. Do not let her think for one more minute she is nothing but a means to an end for you. You know it. I know it. Her father knows it. Hell, I bet even Chase Carter knows it. The only one who doesn't know is the one who needs to. You wait too long, and I swear I'll introduce her to my nephew," Agent Johnson said with a chuckle.

I waited for what seemed an eternity for his response. Could Agent Johnson be right? Could Gabe really love me? It was so quiet the sound of someone blowing out a loud breath startled me.

"Mind your own damn business, Pops," Gabe snapped. "There's no way in hell I'd ever allow that nephew of yours near Karsyn or Abby, so just get that idea out of your head. Right now, I just want this whole assignment behind us. I want Chase Carter behind bars, so they'll be safe. Now if you'll excuse me, I need to tell Mr. McKenna he can go visit his daughter, and then I'm going to catch a few winks before I take a shift outside."

I heard Gabe's footsteps leave the room and head down the other hallway to where he'd settled my father. I leaned against the wall, closed my eyes, and put my hand over my heart. I could feel it pounding in my chest.

"Did you get all that, Mrs. Carter?" Agent Johnson chuckled.

I jumped, startled. My cheeks flushed in embarrassment at being caught eavesdropping. Agent Johnson was standing in front of me, smiling.

"I've known Gabe a long time. He has his own reasons for needing to see this all the way through before he can focus on anything else, but I promise you, he loves you and that little girl of his. I don't want you to give up on him. I know you've got no reason to believe me based on his actions, but try. Try to see beyond what's on the surface," he said, giving me a smile.

I stepped forward and hugged him tightly.

"Thank you, Agent Johnson. I appreciate what you're doing, but I've learned the hard way that happy endings exist only in fairytales. Real life is never that easy. We have a lot to talk about and deal with. I've made mistakes, and he hasn't been honest with me. Abby is all that matters to me, now. I've already given her a monster for a father. I won't make another mistake with her life. I only hope he can forgive me for keeping her from him."

He patted my back and chuckled. "I think you've earned the right to call me Pops. Why don't you head back and check on that little girl of yours. Your father should be along shortly. Wouldn't want Gabe to catch us conspiring in the hallway." He gave me a wink.

"Thank you again…Pops." I smiled. "And please call me Karsyn."

I turned and went back to my room and my daughter, feeling much better. I would give Gabe the time he needed. I would do whatever he needed and help any way I could to help him close his case, not only for Justin and Heather, but for my daughter and the father she needed to know.

Chapter Nineteen

I had just got back into my room and was about to shut the door when I heard my father's voice behind me.

"Kari?"

I turned to find him standing in the hall, shifting his feet and looking uncertain. A smile broke out on my face, and I ran to him.

"Daddy!" I yelled as I threw my arms around him.

I started crying when those warm, protective arms, which had held me through nightmares, bumps and bruises, and Gran's death wrapped around me, cocooning me in their shelter again. As I clung to him, that familiar peace washed over me reminding me how safe he made me feel as a child, the sense that nothing could hurt me. He was strong enough to fight the monsters under the bed or in the closet. He always made sure I knew he loved me and kept me safe. I hadn't realized until this moment just how much I missed being held. I wanted to be Daddy's little girl again and crawl into his lap and let him kiss all the hurt away. How had I let us get so far apart?

"Oh, God, Kari. My baby girl. I thought I'd never see you again." He held me at arm's length looking me over. "Are you okay? I'm so, so sorry I didn't protect you better. I failed you. I hope you can find it in your heart to forgive me one day," he cried.

I stared up at him through tear-filled eyes. I couldn't get over the changes in his appearance. He looked older, worn down, more so than I remembered. His light brown hair was sprinkled with gray now. His hazel eyes had lost their sparkle, and he had dark circles under them, all because of me. I shook my head at him in denial.

"Daddy, I love you. You've never failed me. You've always been there for me. I'm the one who's sorry. I should have listened. I should have believed you instead of letting Chase fill my head with lies. Can you ever forgive me for disappointing you?" I stressed.

He pressed my head against his chest and hugged me tighter before leading me back into my room. We sat on the small sofa across from the bed so I could keep an eye on my sleeping daughter.

"You didn't disappoint me, Kari. Don't ever think that. You're the best daughter any father could ask for. I've loved you from the moment the doctor placed you in my arms, and I'll continue to love you until my last breath on this earth. I've had a lot of time to think about things, and I've come to realize that I made a lot of mistakes while you were growing up. I thought I was protecting you, but now I know all I did was make it easier for him to suck you in."

"I don't understand."

He leaned forward and propped his elbows on his knees, rubbing his face in his hands.

"I need to explain some things to you. You know I met your mom when I had my appendix removed at the same hospital where she worked. What you didn't know is your mother was friends with Chase's mother in school. We lived in Dallas after we got married until we found out she was pregnant. She wanted to move back; she thought it was better to raise kids in a small town than the big city. „Better the devil you know,' she always said, and she had a point. I've always known who and what the Carters really were, but I stayed out of their

132

way and kept my nose out of their business. I did what I thought I needed to in order to keep you and your mom safe. After she died, I thought about moving away, but your grandmother didn't want to leave, and I already had the business established. The Carters left us alone so figured we'd be fine."

"Then he came home with you. He told me he planned to marry you. He didn't want you leaving town. I couldn't stop him on my own. If anything happened to me, it would have left you completely alone. I had to find a way to stop it from happening without Chase knowing. All those doctor appointments were also meetings with the FBI and DEA. They've been trying to bring down the Carters for years. I told them everything I knew and helped set up the cover for one of their agents to work for me."

He stopped at this point in his story to look at me carefully. I nodded my head in understanding. I knew Gabe was an agent, but it still hurt, knowing that dating me was just part of his cover.

"I'm sorry, Kari. I never meant for you to get hurt. If I'd known what was happening, I would have found a way to send you away. All I wanted to do was keep Chase Carter as far away from you as I possibly could. I couldn't stand the idea I'd worked so hard for eighteen years keeping you safe only to have you end up right in the middle of their world, married to the bastard. I didn't want that for you, Kari. I wanted you to have the love and security of a good honest man, a man who would protect you with his life. Instead, you ended up right where I never wanted you to be."

"I went to Gabe's after you left the house that night. Something just didn't feel right to me. I saw your car out front and that girl leaving his house with Bobby and some other guy. I was terrified what I would find inside. I found Gabe drugged and passed out cold on the floor but no sign of you other than your purse on the floor."

"What? What do you mean he was drugged?" I interrupted. My eyes narrowed in confusion.

My dad took both my hands in his and sighed. "Kari, Chase drugged Gabe when they met that night at his club. I found him on the floor of his bedroom. I called an ambulance because nothing would wake him. The hospital confirmed it."

I closed my eyes against the pain. The only reason I married Chase was because I thought Gabe cheated on me. There was no guarantee Gabe and I would have ended up any differently than we were now, but Chase would never have been a part of Abby's life. I wouldn't have spent the last year living a nightmare. My stomach twisted in knots when I remembered Gabe had tried to tell me and I wouldn't listen.

"He never cheated on me," I whispered sadly. "All this time I thought—" I took a deep breath and shook my head to clear it. It still didn't change anything between us. I couldn't allow myself to dwell on this. I was still just a convenience while he was in town; nothing more. I nodded to Dad that I was okay for him to continue.

"I went nuts trying to find you. I drove out to Chase's ranch, but his men wouldn't let me through the gates. I knew I couldn't take them, so I went back to call Gabe's supervisor, and he called in backup."

He pulled me into a hug, and I rested my head on his chest as I hugged him back.

"By the time we got there, it was too late. You were already gone. I had no idea what happened to you or where to even start looking. Then when you called… and he told me he'd bring you home soon... I didn't know whether to feel relief or terror."

I sat up and wiped away my tears.

"I'm so sorry for putting you through that, Daddy. I'm sorry I didn't listen to you and Gabe when you told me to stay away from him. I always listened to you. I don't know why I didn't about Chase. I put you through so much, more than any father should have to," I said sadly.

He shushed me and pulled me back into a hug.

"Don't apologize, Kari. I sheltered you and let you spend time with him over the years. You thought he was your friend and had no reason to think otherwise. That's my fault. I should have kept you away from him, but I thought by allowing the friendship, it would actually make them less inclined to drag you into their world. I should have realized I was basically handing you over to him." He paused a moment, then shifted me to look up at him. "I've asked before, but I need to ask you again. Is Abby his daughter?"

I pulled away and sat up, looking over to the bed where she was starting to fidget in her sleep. She would be awake soon. I smiled at her before turning back to my dad. I shook my head at him.

"No, Daddy. She's Gabe's daughter. I'm sorry I lied to you, but Chase made me promise not to tell anyone." I blew out my breath and pushed my hair away from my face nervously. "I need to talk to Gabe. He knows the truth, and I need to know what he plans to do. I only hope he doesn't try to take her from me when this is over. I don't think it would be hard, considering I lied about her parentage and am married to a drug dealer and murderer. I wouldn't give me custody at this point."

"Do you love him?" he asked carefully.

"Which one?" I smirked wryly. "Chase, not anymore. I did in the beginning, not like I loved Gabe, but more out of friendship and gratitude."

"Gratitude?"

"Daddy, please try and understand. I was so insecure; every boyfriend I ever had dumped me. Then to walk in on Gabe in bed with Brandi, thinking he cheated on me. I didn't know Chase was behind all of it. I thought there must be something wrong with me, that there was something completely unlovable about me for every guy to treat me that way."

"Chase made me feel special, loved. He was a huge boost for my insecurity. He really loved Abby and me. Nothing touched us until I overheard him in his office. I never knew I was married to a monster. He was so good at pretending, that even when little things would slip on occasion, I either overlooked them or would believe his explanation. I was so stupid when I overheard him talking about cocaine on our honeymoon. I believed him when he said I misunderstood the dialect. I was a fool, and I'll be paying for my mistakes for the rest of my life." My breath hitched as I fought back a sob.

"I'm the reason you were hurt. I'm the reason Heather is dead. I'm the reason Abby thinks that monster is her father. I'm so sorry, Daddy, for everything."

"Kari, none of that was your fault; you need to stop blaming yourself," he said sternly. "Chase Carter is to blame for my injuries and Heather's death. I kept you in the dark and that's my fault. You made choices and decisions without knowing the facts. When you found out the truth, you tried to put a stop to him. You did everything you could. You warned me and got me out of there before his men showed up at the house. You tried to escape with Abby to protect her, and we failed you. Gabe still isn't sure how Chase found you. And when you testify to that grand jury in a few weeks, it will be because of you he spends the rest of his life behind bars or they shove a needle in his arm. Without you, he will get away with everything he's done. I'm so proud of you, Karsyn. You alone are putting a stop to one of the biggest drug operations in the state of Texas and years of extortion and murder in our town."

I smiled at him through my sobs as we hugged tightly. "Thank you, Daddy. I love you, and I hope I always make you proud of me from now on."

"And what about Gabe?" he asked gently. "How do you feel about him?" He raised my chin and gave me a sad, knowing smile.

"I never stopped loving Gabe, Daddy. I just want the chance to make things right with him when this is over. I want Abby to know her real father, and I hope he can forgive me. I hope he wants to be a part of her life and lets me continue to be her mother. I don't know what I'd do without Abby. I love her so much. I want to be a good mother and protect her, just like you always did for me."

I went to the bed and picked up Abby, who was now awake and sitting up, staring at us. I kissed her head and rubbed my nose in her hair, smelling her innocent baby smell. I grabbed a diaper from her diaper bag and changed her. I walked back to sit beside my dad. He rubbed her back and made faces at her, coaxing a smile as she tucked her head under my chin and stared at him shyly. She didn't remember him, but she would soon. I also hoped, one day soon, she would know Gabe as her father and forget all about the monster I had brought into our lives.

Chapter Twenty

I smiled as I felt the weight of Abby crawling on my chest. Her little hands pulled at the locket I wore around my neck, which held the pictures of the people she knew and loved. The necklace had belonged to my mother, and I treasured it. I lifted her to sit up and leaned against the headboard with her in my lap. I gently pried it out of her hands and opened it for her.

"Momma," she said, pointing to the picture inside. She bent forward and gave me a wet kiss on my jaw.

"That's right, and who is Momma holding?" I asked, playing the familiar game with her.

"Baby Abby," she smiled.

I skipped the part of the game where she would identify Chase in the picture.

When this is over, I will need to get a new picture taken of us to replace the family picture of Chase and me with Abby. I thought to myself. I even gave myself a brief moment to hope Gabe might want to be in the new picture.

"And who is this?" I pointed to the opposite picture in the locket. It was a picture of my parents on their wedding day.

"Papa!" she said loudly and clapped her hands.

I laughed and hugged her tight. After spending time with the two of us together and constantly referring to him as Papa, it had only taken a day and a half for Abby to remember my dad. We've been together for a week, the longest I've been able to spend with her since I first tried to escape. If it wasn't for the constant threat hanging over our heads, I would be in heaven.

My dad and I spent time reminiscing about the past and rebuilding the relationship we had before Chase. We were growing even closer than we ever were before. He no longer talked to me as his little girl. There was no need to protect me from the big bad world. I lived right in the middle of it. We were on equal footing now, and we talked as adults.

Abby had the agents wrapped around her little finger, too. With me, they kept their distance and stayed professional, but not with Abby. I would often find her bouncing on a knee, playing horsey with whoever was on duty inside the house. Pops had been the first to break. After getting supplies in town, he produced a doll and a small swing, which he tied in a tree out back. "Kids need toys and sunshine," was his gruff reply when I kissed his cheek in thanks. The other agents took that as a sign it was okay to act human and see who could make Abby laugh the loudest.

The only downside, besides the obvious, was the distance that still existed between Gabe and me. I knew he watched Abby and I during the odd moments he would actually be inside with us. He avoided being alone with me for any length of time, always taking the patrols outside. But after what happened last night, I wasn't sure what to think anymore. I was singing Abby to sleep when I noticed him.

I gently stroked Abby's face with my fingers, working at getting her to close her eyes and keep them closed so she would fall asleep. I glanced up as a shadow blocked the crack of light coming from the partially opened bedroom door. I stopped singing as I waited to see what he would do, but Abby began to stir again.

I continued to hum the song to her until she was asleep, knowing Gabe stood at the door the whole time. When she was finally out, I looked over at him again. I couldn't make out his features with the light from the hallway behind him, but I saw his body shift. He took two hesitant steps into the room before I heard his growl of frustration. He turned and left, pulling the door closed behind him.

"Sweet dreams," he whispered before the door clicked closed.

I smiled at the memory as the tug on my necklace brought me back to the present. I wrapped my hand around Abby's to keep her from breaking the chain. She'd done it before, and Chase had gotten it fixed for me. It was the only nice thing he'd done for me during the time he kept me drugged at the house.

"Not so hard, baby." I kissed her forehead and snapped the locket closed. I changed her diaper and got us dressed for the day.

"Let's go get some breakfast in that tummy." I lifted her in the air so I could blow raspberries on her stomach, making her squeal. She clutched the hair at my scalp in her small fists, making me wince. "Ow, Abby, baby, that hurts."

I had my head tucked down as I tried to pry her hands loose without losing my hair when I felt other hands covering mine. I couldn't look up yet, so I stayed still while they helped.

"Abby, don't pull Mommy's hair. It's too pretty. We don't want to hurt Mommy." He paused before he whispered the words I longed to hear, "We love Mommy." He gently pried her little fingers away.

My hands stilled at his voice, and I closed my eyes against the prick of tears behind them. With the last of my hair free, I looked up to see love in Gabe's eyes. I gave him a tentative smile while my lower lip trembled. He stroked my cheek with his fingertip and smiled in return.

"Good morning," I breathed.

"Good morning to you, too," he said with a smile. "Breakfast is ready."

"Do you want to take Abby?" I offered hesitantly.

I didn't know how far to go with this sudden change and I didn't want to assume anything.

He looked at her with wide eyes, and his Adam's apple bobbed as he swallowed hard, but he reached for her and lifted her into his arms. They stared at one another for a minute while Abby sized him up, deciding if he was friend or foe. He pulled out a pocket watch and showed it to her, glancing at me quickly and giving me a gentle smile. I gasped as I recognized the watch I had purchased for him for Christmas that year. Not only did he have the watch, he kept it with him.

"You like shiny things, don't you?"

I smiled when she reached for it and settled into his arms, accepting him as a friend. He visibly relaxed and tightened his arms around her. He kissed her hair and looked over her head at me. I saw the unshed tears in his eyes even as my vision blurred with my own.

"Why don't you take her to the kitchen? I'll be there in a minute."

He swallowed again and nodded before turning and walking out of the room with our daughter. I sat on the side of my bed and forced myself to calm down. My heart was pounding in my chest, but I was afraid to get my hopes up too much. When I had a grip on my emotions, I got up and headed for the kitchen.

I smiled when I saw Abby sitting on Gabe's lap as he fed her bites of scrambled eggs and applesauce while she played with his watch.

My dad was drinking coffee and talking about cars with Agent Adams across the table, seemingly ignoring them to give Gabe time with his daughter. When I entered, Dad looked up and winked at me before shifting his gaze to Gabe. He looked back to me, smiling. Dad cleared his throat and stood, walking over to put his cup in the sink.

"Why don't I take Abby outside, so she can play on the swing for a little while?"

He took Abby from Gabe and handed him back the pocket watch before he and Agent Adams left through the kitchen door. I went to the stove and grabbed a tortilla, filling it with the scrambled eggs and a couple of strips of bacon. Too nervous to sit, I leaned against the counter as I ate my breakfast taco. Gabe finished his coffee, picked up Abby's plate, and put it in the sink beside me. He stood staring out the window at my dad pushing Abby in her swing. We could hear her laughter coming through the open window.

"Your dad said she doesn't like bananas," he said, breaking the uneasy silence between us.

"No, I think it's the texture that bothers her," I replied, looking at him curiously as he nodded.

"I don't like them either." His eyes cut in my direction before staring out the window again.

I smiled, understanding. "That's something you have in common, then," I said gently. "She has your eyes too."

He smiled as he continued to watch her.

"She loves chocolate and old country music like Patsy Cline." I paused and cleared the lump in my throat, causing him to turn to me. "I haven't spent a lot of time with her over the last few months, but Chase said she likes Big Bird from Sesame Street."

I walked away from him and went to curl up on the sofa in the living room. I took several deep breaths to keep myself from crying. He followed and sat in awkward silence beside me for a few minutes while I got control of my emotions. I knew it paled in comparison to how he must feel, having missed everything. I wiped my face and turned to him.

"Gabe—"

"Karsyn, don't. It's not necessary," he interrupted as he brushed his hand across my cheek. He gave me a sad smile. "I forget he took her from you, too."

I shook my head at him and pulled away to stand.

"No, I have to say this. I owe you this and so much more." I sighed as I blew out my breath. I paced in front of the sofa trying to work off my nervous energy.

"Karsyn," he tried again.

I walked back over and sat down beside him, putting my fingers over his mouth to stop him.

"Please, just let me say this. Please?" I begged.

He sighed in resignation and nodded his head. As I pulled my fingers away, he reached for my hand and held it in his. I stared down and watched as his thumb brushed over my knuckles.

"I am so sorry. I'm sorry for not believing in you and running instead of staying and fighting for us. That night...I knew in my heart you wouldn't cheat on me, but I didn't listen to it. I let my insecurities overshadow all else. I listened to Chase's lies, and they fed that insecurity until I lost all faith in us. I let him overwhelm and take me over so I wouldn't have to think about my pain. I was scared and I thought I was alone." I looked up at him and felt the tears spill onto my hand.

"I can never tell you how sorry I am that I brought Chase into Abby's life. Please, don't take her from me. I love Abby with all my heart, and I'll do anything if you'll just please let me continue to be in her life. I can't live without her again. I want you to know her. I want Abby to know you're her father, whatever you want. Just please, don't take her from me."

"Are you done now?" he asked, smiling.

I nodded nervously, not understanding the smile and swallowed.

He released my hand and slid his hand around my neck, pulling me to him as he leaned in.

"I would never take Abby from you. I've watched you with her this week, and you're a wonderful mother. Thank you for loving my daughter the way you do. I just need to know one thing." His breath caressed my face with just the barest whisper of his lips against mine.

"Wha—what do you want to know?" I breathed as my eyes closed. I strained to bridge the last small space between us.

"Can you honestly say you love me even without knowing who I really am?" he asked gently.

My eyes opened to see the love and vulnerability I knew matched my own in his eyes. I touched his face and smiled. I felt like I would burst, my emotions were so overwhelming. The bonds I had kept wrapped so tightly around my heart all this time broke free as the tears ran, unchecked, down my face.

"But, I do know you. I know you're honest and driven by what's right. You love passionately. Your jaw twitches when you're angry, and your left eye crinkles in the corner when you're happy. I know you're a bear in the mornings before you've had at least two cups of coffee, and I never felt more loved or safer than being held in your arms at night." I took a breath before continuing.

"There's a lot that I don't know about who you really are, but I know what matters the most and I should have never lost sight of that. I love you, Gabriel Thompson—mechanic, agent, or whatever else you may be. It doesn't matter to me. You're a good man either way. I have a lot of work to do to earn your trust and respect, but if you want my blind faith, you have it."

He leaned away from me and shook his head.

"I don't want your blind faith, Karsyn. I want you to trust me with both eyes open and knowing the truth. Asking for your blind faith was wrong of me. I demanded your trust without ever giving you a reason to trust me. I lied to you about who I was, making me no better than Chase Carter. I promise when this is over, I'll work to earn your trust. I want you, and I want my daughter. I may have lied about everything else, but I never lied about my feelings for you. I lo—"

The sound of gunfire and Abby's terrified cries coming from outside drowned out the rest of Gabe's speech.

Chapter Twenty One

"Abby!" I screamed. I leapt from the sofa only to have Gabe shove me to the ground and cover me with his body.

"Stay down!"

The living room windows shattered, raining glass down on us. I felt the burn of tiny cuts on my arms and legs. I struggled against him, trying in vain to get up.

"Abby and Dad are out there! I have to get to them!"

"I know, damn it!" He pushed me ahead of him as we crawled to hide behind the sofa. "Adams! Johnson! Martinez! Somebody, fucking talk to me!" he shouted into his radio.

"We're a little busy out here. There's a fucking shit storm raining down on us out here. Schmidt's dead and Martinez took a hit in the side. We're pinned in the front. I haven't heard from Adams or Martin in the back, but they gotta be just as pinned as we are," Pops' strained voice answered.

Gabe shifted before pulling the couch cushions on top of me. The sound of gunfire surrounded us as glass shattered throughout house. I screamed and sobbed as I pictured my baby and dad outside, defenseless. Were they still alive? I strained to listen and felt a flicker of hope when I recognized her cries mixed with the sounds of the firestorm of bullets.

"Don't move from this spot, do you understand me?"

"Abby and my dad," I cried, staring at him through wide, fearful eyes.

I was shaking and my teeth chattered. Adrenaline pumped furiously through my body. My only thoughts centered on getting to Abby and my dad. I tried again, unsuccessfully, to rise. I screamed and clutched frantically at his shirt as a bullet hit the television set nearby, causing it to explode.

"Karsyn, damn it, I need to get outside! I can't do my job if I'm worried about you too, baby. Stay down behind the sofa and keep these cushions over you." Reaching down, he pulled a small handgun from his ankle holster and pushed it into my shaking fingers. "If anyone you don't know comes through that door, you shoot. The safety's off; you just pull the trigger."

I nodded my understanding as he pressed an urgent kiss to my forehead.

"Please be safe."

"I will. I'm going to get Abby and your dad. Stay here."

He pulled away from me and crawled out of the room toward the kitchen. As more bullets hit the wall behind me, I screamed and tucked my head against my chest. Chunks of sheetrock pelted the cushions covering me. I lifted the corner of the cushion to track Gabe's progress but could no longer hear or see him. He must have made it out of the house.

I gripped the gun in my sweaty hands, trying not to think about the possibility of shooting someone. I'd never held a gun before. I'd never gone hunting with my dad when I was younger, and Chase never let me near them after we were married.

I closed my eyes and focused on Abby's cries outside. As long as I could hear her, I knew she was alive.

It seemed like forever before I realized the shooting had stopped. I heard a helicopter descending and held my breath, waiting. I strained to hear Gabe or anyone telling me it was safe to come out. I could still hear Abby crying outside. She must be terrified. Gabe told me to stay put, but I needed to go to her. We had to be safe if the shooting stopped, didn't we?

I pushed the cushions covered in glass and sheetrock off me and pushed my hair from my face as I sat up. I listened for any indication he was bringing Abby to me.

"Karsyn! You can come out, love!"

I froze in fear at the voice calling me.

"Karsyn! Our daughter needs you!"

"No. No. No," I whispered in desperation.

I closed my eyes and shook my head in denial. I knew when the shooting started that Chase was behind it, but I never stopped to think he would actually be here. If he had Abby, he had me and he knew it.

"Karsyn! Now, love! You don't want to be responsible for another death, do you?" Chase shouted angrily.

I pushed myself up from the ground and surveyed the destruction around me. Bullet holes riddled the walls and glass and sheetrock littered the floor. In the kitchen, an upper cabinet door had splintered and twisted, hanging by one hinge. I sprinted to the back door, slipping on broken glass and debris, and froze in the doorway. Chase was standing in the yard with Abby, bouncing her on his hip and trying to calm her cries as she clung to him. He held a gun in his other hand, pointed at Gabe who was kneeling in front of him with his hands behind his head. Pops and three other agents were in similar positions at the corner of the house with a couple of Chase's men standing over them.

"Chase! Please don't. I'm coming," I begged as I stepped outside.

"Look, Abby. Here comes Mommy. Don't worry, sweetie, Mommy and Daddy are going to get you home where you belong," he grinned, staring at me. His gaze flickered down to Gabe in front of him, and he laughed. "Problem, Agent Thompson?"

My eyes frantically swept the yard searching for my dad as I made my way outside to Chase. The swing Abby had been happily playing in just a short time ago hung by one rope as it swayed awkwardly in the air from the turning blades of the helicopter. The other rope draped across the back of Agent Adams lying face down on the ground, dead. I looked beyond the swing and cried out in horror.

"Daddy!" I ran to the edge of the tree line and dropped to my knees, grabbing his shoulder to turn him over. It was hopeless. He was gone. I threw myself across his body and held him tightly. I would never again feel his strong arms hold me or comfort me. He would never again say he loved me. "Daddy, please don't leave me! I need you!" I sobbed.

I fought against the rough hands that pulled me up and shoved me toward Chase. I twisted free, straightening my shoulders and holding my head up high. I walked back to Chase, keeping my eyes on Abby. I tried not to look at Gabe as I walked past him, but failed.

"Karsyn, don't," he begged.

I fell to my knees in front of him and let him wrap me in his arms. I needed this moment, knowing it could very well be our last.

"I love you Gabe. I've always loved you," I whispered urgently.

"Everything will be okay. I love—" Gabe began.

I cried as one of Chase's men pulled me away from him. Emotion flickered in Gabe's eyes, and he smiled reassuringly before he stared up at Chase again.

"Excuse me, Agent Thompson, but I don't think you're in a position to order my wife to do anything," Chase laughed darkly.

"I will hunt you down if it's the last thing I do! I will get my daughter and Karsyn back."

Chase laughed again and fired a shot at Gabe, hitting the ground next to him and spraying dirt over him.

"Chase, please don't," I begged, running forward to stand between them. "I'll go with you. Just please, don't hurt anyone else! Not in front of Abby!"

He raised his gaze to me, and I saw the promise of retribution in his eyes. My life was about to become a bigger hell than ever. He tsked and shook his head at me. He let me take Abby from him but tucked me against his side, holding me firmly against him. I worked to calm Abby as her screams had left her hoarse, and her hiccupping only led to more sobs.

"Karsyn, Karsyn. What am I going to do with you? You promised ,til death do us part,' remember? I warned you, I would never let you go, and I would always find you."

"How did you find her? Did you pay off someone on my team?" Gabe demanded.

I knew Chase would never let Gabe or the other agents live. I wracked my brain for some way to bargain for their lives, but came up with nothing. Chase held all the cards now. He had me. He had Abby. There was nothing else he cared about.

Chase shrugged. "Actually, no, I didn't. It wasn't necessary. All I had to do was sit back and wait for you to bring Abby and Karsyn together." He laughed at the matching stares of confusion Gabe and I shared. "You agents always underestimate me. You think you can second-guess me. If that were the case, you'd have caught me long before now. Hell, this was actually easier than getting that whore, Brandi, to make it look like you were having sex with her. You were so out of it; you didn't even know what was going on around you. Still, it got the job done, and you, Karsyn, came running straight to me, just as I knew you would."

I gasped in fear as Chase reached forward with the gun still in his hand and grabbed my locket, yanking the chain until it snapped.

"What? Did you think I was going to hurt you? Relax, love." He reached up and brushed the barrel of his gun against my cheek, laughing as I froze in fear. "When are you going to realize, I love you, Karsyn. I would never hurt my wife or the mother of my children."

"You son of a bitch!" Gabe snarled as he tried to lunge at Chase.

Chase quickly cocked his gun aiming it at Gabe's head. One of Chase's thugs hit Gabe with his gun, knocking him to the ground again. I screamed and tucked Abby's face against my chest. I hated all the violence her young mind was witnessing today. Gabe struggled to gain his balance again. A gash on his temple oozed blood, and I buried my face in Abby's hair to hide my own tears at the sight.

"Now, before I was so rudely interrupted," Chase laughed, mockingly. "I can see you've guessed how I found Karsyn. She never took off this locket." He held it up. "All I had to do was wait for the tracking device hidden inside and the other device sewn into Abby's diaper bag to come together."

"You should have realized I would never make it that easy for you to take my wife and daughter. But I would never risk my family's safety, either. I instructed my men to let you leave if you got close enough to grab them."

"You risked her safety and Karsyn's today, you bastard," Gabe snarled. "What does that say for your holier-than-thou attitude?"

"Ah, but I knew you would do everything in your power to protect my family, Agent Thompson. They were never in any real danger."

"What about Karsyn's father? Doesn't that go against your supposed vow of not hurting Karsyn?" Gabe sneered. "Where's your smug justification in that? What about the agents you killed today who she called „friend'?"

I shook my head at him. He was provoking Chase, and I had no idea how he would react.

"Gabe, don't. I can't lose you, too."

Chase growled at my words and grabbed my arm in his fierce grip. His face twisted in anger as he stared down at me.

"Take Abby and get in the helicopter. You had better wipe your mind clear of your agent, right now," he ordered. "You're my wife, and you will never be given another chance to escape me."

I raised my chin and stared back into his eyes, conveying all the hatred I felt for him. My father was dead, and I was about to lose Gabe forever. Abby had lost her grandfather and was about to lose her father just as she was beginning to know him. I summoned all the courage I had within me and spit in his face.

"I loathe you, Chase Carter. I hope you rot in hell. I will hate you until my last breath on this earth. I never stopped loving Gabe, and I will always love him. I may be trapped with you, but you will only feel my contempt. I love Gabe, and I will find a way for Abby and I to get back to him one day," I vowed.

His eyes darkened at my words, and his lips slowly widened into an evil smile. He held my arm as he pulled me over to the helicopter and wrenched open the door. He took Abby from me and pushed me inside before handing her back to me. I ignored the pilot sitting in the front as I stared at Chase with fearful eyes.

"You'll never leave me if there's no one to come back to, will you? I should have done this from the very beginning," he said darkly.

He stepped back and cocked his gun as he turned back to Gabe. I put Abby behind me on the bench seat and faced my husband for, hopefully, the last time.

"Chase, darling," I called.

He looked back at me, startled by my sweet tone of voice. His eyes widened in surprise as he noticed what was in my hands. I squeezed the trigger and jumped at how loud the shot sounded within the tight quarters of the helicopter. I registered the sound of another gun rapidly firing outside as Chase fell. I turned quickly to the pilot and pointed the gun at him. My hand shook, but I held my ground as I pulled Abby back into my lap, trying to soothe her again.

"Please don't make me shoot you too, Mr. Kent," I said shakily as I stared at the back of his head. I hoped he didn't turn around to see how unsteady my hand was. I probably wouldn't be able to pull the trigger again if I tried. I swallowed hard at his deep chuckle.

"Damn, girl. I would have never guessed you had the guts to actually pull the trigger. I always figured you were just window dressing. No need to get antsy, I'm just sitting here," he smirked.

"Karsyn, it's alright, baby. You can let go now," Gabe said gently. His hand covered mine as he took the gun. He helped me get out of the helicopter before enfolding Abby and I in a tight embrace. I closed my eyes and soaked up the feeling of being safe in his arms again. "It's over, baby. He can't hurt you anymore."

MICHAEL SCHNEIDER

I saw Chase lying on the ground. Blood seeped into the grass around him from the hole in his neck, a look of surprise frozen on his face in death. I had almost missed, but I was close enough. I shuddered and turned away from him for the last time.

Chapter Twenty Two

Three months later

I sat at the kitchen table and stared into my cooling cup of coffee. I spent most of my nights and early mornings in this position as sleep usually eluded me. I would sit in Abby's room for several hours after she fell asleep before finding my way into the kitchen. The coffee pot would be waiting for me, courtesy of the kind federal agent assigned to watch over us.

One would think we would be safe now with Chase dead, but we weren't. Not yet, anyway. Chase's death did cut off the head of the beast, so to speak, but the body was still alive and fighting for self-preservation. Just two weeks after I buried my dad, I met with the grand jury and gave them everything I knew: names, places, dates. As Chase's widow, I had the authority to open the doors to the company offices and our homes.

The District Attorney was in seventh heaven. His career paved in gold with the convictions he stood to gain from the evidence they had. Evidence they would have never been able to obtain any other way. I never realized how dark and ugly Chase and his father really were. The man I'd known never existed. I had only known the mask he wore for my benefit. Chase was involved in drugs, prostitution, extortion, and more deaths than I could count. I shuddered again as I remembered the details that became known as the investigation continued.

The government confiscated everything Chase owned, which basically left Abby and I homeless, not that I would ever go back to the ranch. I couldn't even go back to my dad's house. I was unwelcome in the town I'd lived in my whole life. Chase's death left no one to blame, and I was guilty by association, if nothing else.

For the first time, people were free to express what they truly felt about the Carters without fear, and they needed someone to direct their anger toward. Heather's parents told me they didn't blame me for her death, but it was easy to see they no longer felt the same way about me. They also needed someone to blame, and I understood that. What no one wanted to remember was that Chase murdered my father, too, and I was as much a victim as they were.

I collected Dad's life insurance and sold his home at a fraction of its worth. I would rebuild our life on this and hoped it was enough. The trust fund Chase set up for Abby couldn't be touched until she turned eighteen. There was another trust for me, but I didn't want to touch it unless I had to. I wanted nothing from him.

I glanced up when I heard the scrape of another cup being pulled from the cabinet.

"Is it an early morning this time, Mrs. Carter, or have you not been to bed yet?" Agent Reed asked. He leaned against the counter and began drinking his coffee, waiting for my answer.

Agent Reed was in his mid-thirties and tall with sandy blonde hair. He and Pops took shifts watching over us. He was polite, but didn't feel the need to get overly chummy. He kept a respectful distance and insisted on calling me Mrs. Carter, no matter how many times I'd asked him to call me by my first name. I hated any reminder of the fact that my life was still tied to Chase and would continue to be so. I already asked the attorneys handling the case if they could get my name changed back to my maiden name, but it wasn't a high priority to anyone but me. So, legally I remained Mrs. Carter, much to my dismay.

I looked out the window at the sky, pink with the beginning of another sunrise. Another day of waiting. Waiting to live or waiting to die; I wouldn't know until Gabe came home. I still didn't know where we stood, and my life was in limbo until then.

"I guess time got away from me again," I offered with a shrug.

"It'll be over soon," he replied kindly.

"I know," I sighed. "I just wish I knew what happens next. Have you heard anything on Agent Thompson?"

Gabe moved Abby and I to another safe house after that fateful day. We were now residing in a huge house in an exclusive gated community outside of DC. It was so much more than I ever imagined a safe house would be. I thought all safe houses were small out of the way places like the cabin we had been in before. This felt like a home, though, despite its size. I'd settled into a large bedroom on the second floor next to Abby's room. With its king size bed covered in deep reds and creams, I actually felt at home. The antique furnishings throughout the house were dark cherry or mahogany and obviously expensive. The day we moved in, a jungle gym for Abby to play on was delivered and set up in the backyard. It was easy to pretend Abby and I lived here in this safe little world where nothing could touch us. The only thing missing was Gabe.

"I'm sure he's fine. Agent Thompson is known for thinking quick on his feet, and he's pulled my ass out of the fire enough times," he laughed. "I tell you, he's probably got more lives than your cat," he said, pointing to Cola, the Himalayan curled at my feet.

She had been a gift from Gabe, along with a well-trained silver Keeshond named Risk, who slept in Abby's room at night. Where I was a cat person, Abby was a dog person, something else she obviously inherited from Gabe. He brought the dog with him the day after we settled into the house and introduced him to Abby before he left again.

They've been inseparable ever since. Gabe assured me Abby was perfectly safe with the dog and that Keeshonds were one of the best breeds to have around children. The dogs were affectionate, extremely loyal, and protective. He said Risk would never allow anyone to harm Abby or me.

"Do you think it would be alright to get a small Christmas tree to put up or to go to a store and get a couple of things for Abby to open?"

Christmas was only two days away, and I hated the idea of her not having anything to mark the day. Thanksgiving had been dismal with no one to share it with except Agent Reed. Being single, he'd elected to stay with us that day so Pops could spend time with his family for the holiday. I didn't know when Gabe would return or what would happen when he did. We still hadn't really talked. He loved Abby and me, and I clung to that and the hope that he wanted to build a family with us when this was over.

"I'm sure we can come up with something for you, but I don't think it's a good idea for you to be out and about just yet. Maybe if you tell me what you want, I can have someone pick it up with the next grocery delivery. I'm sorry; I know this is tough on you, but it won't be much longer. We just need to round up the last of the key players. You and your daughter should be placed with WITSEC—"

"WITSEC? What is that?" I looked up, startled at his words.

"Witness Security Program. Your new identities should be ready after the holidays."

"Witness Security? No one said anything about us having to change our identities!" My heart began to race. If Abby and I disappeared with new identities, how could we be a family with Gabe? Did he know about this? Is that why he was gone and never mentioned a future with us, because he knew we wouldn't have one?

That son of a bitch! He said, "Trust him," and like an idiot I did. I've sat here for three months making excuses for him, letting his empty words reassure me that everything would work out. I knew he was trying to take down the last of Chase's organization, and that's why I hadn't heard from him. But now I wondered, was it also so he wouldn't have to face me again?

"It's standard procedure in a case this big; even if the key players are behind bars, they could still get to you. It may take years before all the convictions are finalized with the appeals and everything. Plus, they'll still have their minions on the outside to do their dirty work. We'll get everyone we can, but there are always those who slip through the cracks. I'm sorry, but you can't just move into a little suburb and go on with your life. It would be too dangerous. I don't think you realize how easy it would be for someone to track you down."

I closed my eyes and shook my head in resignation. "We're never going to be safe, are we?" I said flatly. I pushed back from the table and stood. "I think I'm going to check on Abby, and then I might lie down for a while."

"I'm sorry if I upset you, Mrs. Carter. That wasn't my intention. Trust me; we're going to do everything we can to keep you and your little girl safe. I just thought you should know the facts. I don't know why no one bothered to tell you before."

I left the kitchen and trudged slowly up the stairs. My mind was numb and couldn't process the information I'd just been told. I checked on Abby, who was still sleeping, and petted Risk's head as he got up at the sound of my entrance. He was alert and tense until he recognized me.

"Thank you for keeping watch," I whispered. I was rewarded with a wet tongue licking my hand before he lay back down beside her crib.

I went into my room and crawled in the bed. I stared at the ceiling and let my mind drift again to thoughts of Gabe, as it always did. Was he safe? Did he think about us? Did he miss us as much as I missed him? Would I get to see him again before they came to take Abby and I away? Would he know where they moved us? And lastly, would he even care? I rolled over and pulled the blanket over my head trying to hide from my life.

Ↄ ⁊

I must have slept, because I opened my eyes, unsure of what had awakened me. As soon as I heard the doorbell ring, I jumped to my feet. When I heard the incessant knocking on the door, I rushed down the hall to Abby's room. She was just beginning to stir, so I woke her and got her dressed. I didn't know if something was wrong or who was at the door, but I was learning to be prepared at a moment's notice. I certainly wasn't expecting the sight that greeted me as I came down the stairs.

Agent Reed was holding the door open as a woman in a long wool coat came into the house along with several men in black suits. The men I recognized as being some sort of agents, but the woman had me stumped. She appeared to be in her late forties or early fifties, average height with jet-black hair pulled up in a bun. She seemed to be the one in charge of the entourage entering the house. She stood in the foyer and surveyed her surroundings.

"I knew it! This will not do! Where are they?" she demanded as she turned to Agent Reed.

"Mrs. Carter and her daughter are still upstairs sleeping, Mrs. Wingate. I'm sorry, but I don't understand why you're here or how you even got authorization to be here?" he replied as his brow wrinkled. His confusion was obvious in the slow cautious tone of his response. He evidently knew who they were, or they would have never made it past the guards at the gate, let alone into the house.

"My authorization? Please," she smirked. She reached up and patted his cheek, looking at him as if she were dealing with a child. "You don't worry yourself about my authorization. Just so you know, I have it and intend to use it. I've kept my distance for as long as I'm going to." She waved her hand dismissingly at him.

"You just run along and play with your guns, drink your coffee, or do whatever it is you do all day, just so long as you stay out of our way." She looked up and saw me standing on the stairs with Abby in my arms. Her stern expression softened and broke into a smile as she clapped her hands.

"There she is!" She beckoned me with her hands as she moved to the foot of the stairs. "Come down here and let me get a good look at her."

I descended the stairs hesitantly, not knowing who she was or why she was so excited to see us. When I reached the bottom, she raised her hand and gently brushed Abby's hair from her face, smiling. Her gaze shifted to me. As she looked me over, I felt like I was on trial or facing some sort of test to which I didn't know the question.

"Hello. I'm Karsyn, and this is my daughter, Abby. Are you with Witness Protection? I—I didn't know we would have to leave so soon."

She laughed lightly and shook her head. "Oh no, child, I can assure you I'm not with them. We did come to get you and your darling daughter, though." She laughed kindly at my mistake.

She turned back to Agent Reed, who was talking off to the side with one of the agents who had come in. He appeared stressed about whatever document he was reading.

"I'm sure you've been informed of the change in plans by now. See that their things are moved later today. And you be sure to tell that good for nothing, Agent Thompson, he's in the dog house with me when he gets back. There isn't even a tree for this poor child."

"Excuse me! I don't know who you think you are or where you get your information from, but I'll have you know Gabe is an excellent agent. He's protected us and taken very good care of us. How dare you say anything against him!" I snapped.

I didn't know who she was, but I wasn't going to stand here and listen to her run him down. We may have our own issues to work out, but I still felt the need to defend him for everything he'd done so far. Without Gabe, I'd still be married to Chase, stuck on that godforsaken island, and probably pregnant with his child. I owed Gabe my loyalty for that if nothing else.

"I knew I'd like you. You've got fire in your blood and that's good," she laughed. "You're going to be so good for him."

I stared at her in confusion.

"Who are you?" I demanded.

"Forgive my manners; I'm Cecile Wingate. Now we really must run. Everyone is waiting, and I like to stay on schedule."

The name sounded familiar. I'd heard it before but couldn't figure out where. She wrapped her arm around me, and after bundling Abby against the cold, we were quickly ushered out of the house and into a waiting limousine. Two black SUV's were parked with it, and the agents piled into the vehicles as we pulled out.

We drove for about twenty minutes while she alternated between beaming at us and trying to get Abby to come to her. She refused to say any more about where we were going, saying everything would be explained soon.

I gasped when we pulled through a large gate and onto a private drive. The house we had just left was a shack compared to this one. This mansion was massive and imposing with its three stories of tan brick and slate roof. It was probably well over a hundred years old and preserved with lots of love. And lots of money. With wide eyes, I turned back to the other occupant sitting across from me.

I was stunned, and as we came to a stop, I asked, "Who are you people?"

The door opening prevented her from answering. The same agents helped us out of the car and ushered us into the house. Snippets of conversation and laughter mixed with the soft sounds of classical Christmas music came from down the hall. I stood gaping at my surroundings as a man in a dark suit, who I could only presume was the butler, began helping us out of our coats. Everything was elegant and pristine and very high end. Garlands and flowers draped the massive central staircase that curved up to the second and third floors. A large Christmas tree covered in shimmering white lights and adorned with ribbons and flowers that matched the garland reached beyond the second floor balcony. A chorus of large ceramic angels surrounded the base, their faces raised as if in song. The hall table boasted a beautiful nativity scene, which looked like a family heirloom or antique. The whole place looked like a Christmas wonderland and was something right out of one of my dreams.

"Could you please tell me why we're here, Mrs. Wingate?" I asked, perplexed. I was tired of being kept in the dark. Everyone talked over me or around me, but never really to me. I wanted someone to take the time to sit down with me and answer my questions. I felt like I'd traded one prison built on Chase's lies for another built on half truths and I was getting sick of it.

"Karsyn, dear, please call me Cecile." She smiled warmly at me and put her arm around my shoulders giving me a gentle squeeze. "You're here so you and Abby can have a real Christmas instead of holed up in some empty house. I hate that Daniel couldn't push through all the red tape sooner. We just want to get to know you and this beautiful child better. Trust me; everyone is ecstatic to finally meet you."

"You keep saying ‚trust you,' but I don't even know you," I stressed. "I'm so fed up with everyone keeping things from me. I think I've earned the right to know what's going on. I'm sorry, but right now the only person I trust is me."

She appraised me thoughtfully a moment and pursed her lips before smiling again. "Stubborn, just like he said," she stated mysteriously. "Tell me, do you trust Agent Thompson?"

"Of course," I exclaimed. "I trust him with our lives."

"Well then just know you can trust us as well. We care as much for your safety and happiness as he does."

I ground my teeth in frustration at her words. I was really going to lose it if someone didn't start giving me some answers and soon. I jumped; startled as the double wooden doors slid open next to us, and two men immerged from a study.

"I'm glad you finally see it my way, Jerry. I owe you one."

My gaze shifted between them as I recognized them both. Jerry was actually District Attorney Jeremy Blakely. The other man I recognized from all the news and political talk shows Chase used to watch on television. He was in his early fifties and you could feel the strength and power emanating from him. He was Senator Daniel Wingate and was favored to be the next president. I remembered Chase always ranting and complaining about him. Now, of course, I understood why. Senator Wingate was determined to crush the ever-expanding drug problem in the US.

"Well, now that I have all the facts, I'll make the necessary calls to cancel WITSEC. I agree they couldn't be better protected than here with family. You know, all Gabe had to do was give me the facts. I'm not particularly fond of all his cloak and dagger bullshit. You tell that godson of mine to remember, I'm still family too. You do realize you're a lucky son of a bitch," he said with a chuckle. "Your candidacy is practically guaranteed now." He turned to see me standing there and smiled pleasantly. "Hello, Mrs. Carter."

I instinctively held Abby closer as fear washed over me at whatever unknown threat was hanging over us now. I was afraid of what his being here could mean for me. The only times we'd met previously were to go over any evidence, pick my brain for more details, or to testify. His being in DC could only mean something was wrong. I always flew to Texas to meet, keeping my current location safely hidden.

"Has something happened?" I asked in a panic.

Chapter Twenty Three

"No, nothing's wrong, I promise. Don't worry, it's almost over," he smiled in understanding.

He turned back to Senator Wingate. "Now I better get back in the living room with my lovely wife before she unleashes that famous Irish temper on me for doing business on family time," he chuckled before walking away and disappearing down the hall.

I mumbled a confused goodbye to Mr. Blakely and turned back to the Senator. I was about to ask him why I was here, but the words died on my lips as I stared at him. I saw the same dark eyes and aristocratic nose, the same strong chin. He was broad shouldered with dark brown hair, which was just beginning to grey at the temples. Even the timbre of his voice was the same, now that I was hearing it without the distortion of television. The hair was the only difference.

Before I could voice my suspicions, I was interrupted again, this time by someone coming through the front door. I forgot everything else, and my face lit up as I watched Gabe come in, that was, until I saw the scowl on his face when he saw me.

"Hello, sir. Karsyn?" he said cautiously. His eyes bore into mine, and my smile slipped under the intensity of his stare. Was he not happy to see us? Did he not want us here?

My gaze swiftly shifted at the sound of the Senator's deep laugh beside me.

"Come along, dear. I think its best we leave them to clear the air," he laughed as he held out his hand to his wife. "I look forward to visiting with you soon, Karsyn."

She turned to me. "May I please take Abby into the other room to give you two a few minutes to talk? I promise she'll be right down the hall, and I'll take very good care of her." I saw the longing in her eyes as she reached for Abby. I already suspected who she was. I nodded and coaxed Abby to go with her. The promise of a cookie finally convinced her. Gabe and I needed to talk, and that couldn't be accomplished with Abby in the room.

I wasn't sure what I was feeling just yet and didn't know if I should hug him or hit him once we were alone. "Please just listen to him with an open mind." I could only nod as my mind rushed with questions, excitement, and worry.

She walked up and hugged Gabe, kissing his cheek before stepping away again. She shook her finger at him. "Gabriel, you make this right, whatever you have to do," she admonished before walking away with the senator.

CR SO

Gabe ushered me into the Senator's study and turned to slide the doors closed so we would have some privacy. My gaze took in the masculine feel of the room as I stood in the middle of the burgundy Oriental rug. A large, wooden desk stood with its leather high backed chair and the two smaller matching chairs facing it, the floor to ceiling bookcases filled with legal books. But what caught my attention was the large oil painting hanging above the mantel of the fireplace.

It was a family portrait, which had obviously been done years before, of the senator and his wife, Cecile. Gone were the crinkles around the eyes and the smattering of grey hair on the man I had just met. He and his wife posed on a loveseat, holding hands while the family dog, a keeshond, lay at their feet. Two teenage boys stood behind them while a younger girl perched on the arm of the loveseat next to her mother.

"I was nineteen when the painting was done," he said, coming up beside me. "That's my brother, Richard. He's a year younger than me and a communications specialist with the Navy. He and his fiancée, Lana, are coming in from Virginia tomorrow for Christmas. You'll get to meet them then. And that's my little sister, Katherine. She's a senior at Princeton and is probably out in the hall right now trying to listen through the door."

"I am not!" I heard a feminine voice yell through the door in indignation.

"Katherine Eleanor, get away from that door!" The Senator's deep voice shouted before footsteps walked away.

The silence thickened before I heard his frustrated sigh beside me.

"Karsyn, say something. Anything. Yell and scream at me. Just please baby, tell me what you're thinking."

"Is that Risk?" I asked, pointing at the dog in the painting, choosing the easiest question first.

"No, Risk's father," he sighed again. "Is that really what you want to ask me?"

His hands went to my shoulders and gently turned me to face him. I saw the uncertainty in his eyes as I looked at him. I wasn't sure what I was feeling or thinking. I knew I was about to explode. How could he expect me to process everything and give him a response? I've lived with so many lies and half truths. Now to have this dumped on top of everything else. I decided to go with the most important question of all and see where things went.

"Who are you? Really, this time. No more lies. No more secrets," I demanded.

His eyes softened as a smile slowly spread across his face. He reached up and cupped my face with both hands and brushed his thumbs across my cheeks. My eyes closed briefly and opened again as I let myself soak up the familiar sensation of being held by him. God, I had missed this man, no matter who he was, however, I stiffened my resolve not to crumble and pulled away from him.

His smile vanished, and his arms fell back to his sides. "My name is Gabriel Jefferson Wingate. I'm the eldest son to Senator Daniel and Cecile Wingate and a federal agent with DEA. Gabe Thompson was a ghost identity set up for my cover. He isn't real. I'm sorry for lying to you all those months about who I was, but it—"

"But you were just doing your job. I understand," I said brusquely. I nodded, walked across the room, and stared out at the barren garden beyond covered in snow as I fought to keep my emotions in check. I wasn't sure what to feel.

I knew months ago that he was an agent. It still stung, though, that the man I loved was…what? Not who he said he was? I knew that already. I had already told him none of it mattered; I loved who he was inside. A name was just a name. So why wasn't I in his arms? Why was I holding back from him?

I knew why. Because he still hadn't been honest with me. A year ago I would have taken him at his word and opened my arms and my heart to him. I wasn't that same naïve little girl any longer. I lived through a hell most people never fathom, and I had a child to protect. I would never be that stupid to give my blind faith again. I knew what I needed to ask next and felt the apprehension settle in my chest.

"Was I—" Clearing my throat, I tried again to get the words past my lips. Words that I knew had the power to hurt me or heal me. "Was I just part of your job?" I whispered.

I needed to know. Gabe put his hands on my shoulders turned me to face him. One hand slid down my back to wrap around my waist while the other gently cupped the back of my head, his thumb tilting my face up to meet his gaze. My breath hitched and tears slipped silently down my cheeks as I saw the emotion I longed for in his eyes. A sob broke at his words.

"I may have lied about a lot of things, but I never lied about how I felt. The town was a job. Chase Carter was a job. You were never part of my job. I love you, Karsyn. I've always loved you, and I want to build a life with you and Abby. I want what we should have had from the beginning. No lies. No secrets. Just us. I tried to tell you that at the cabin before all hell broke loose on us."

There was one burning question I needed to have answered. One doubt had plagued my mind since he showed up on that island. It was part of the reason I didn't sleep at night.

"I have to know. Why did you leave us there?" I asked, my anxiety and resentment making heart race. I tried to pull away from him only to have him tighten his arms around me. "Why? If you loved me, and you knew Abby was yours after she was born, why didn't you come for us? You told me you knew. You say you love us, but if that's the case, why didn't you save us?"

"Karsyn, I couldn't, baby. Believe me I wanted nothing more than to take you and Abby away. I love you. She's my daughter, and she calls a criminal Daddy. Do you know how much it killed me knowing he was raising my daughter? That he was touching you, making love to you? You two are everything to me, and that bastard had you both! He had my life!

I was ordered to back off and leave town. Justin was already in place by then, and we needed to get the evidence to bring Chase Carter to justice. The sooner we arrested him, the sooner I could be close to you again. Chase was too cautious of outsiders, which is why he eluded prosecution for so long. The only way for Justin to gain access to the inside was through your friendship with Heather. We had no other way," he said in defeat. "My boss threatened that if I caused any trouble, he'd put me in a prison cell until the case was over and to put you and Abby in Witness Protection where I'd never find you. This case was too big, and it was very personal to my family."

"Why? Because your father is planning to run for president in a couple of years? I'm sure politically it must look pretty good that his son helped bring down Chase Carter's empire," I sneered. I was hurt and angry. I understood most of what he was saying, but that didn't make it any easier to swallow. But to say it was more important to his father's career was like a slap in the face. If that's what mattered to these people, then I wanted no part of them.

He sighed and shook his head at me. "It has absolutely nothing to do with my father's career, Karsyn. Do you remember me telling you about my cousin, and how I looked up to him and admired him?" When I nodded, he continued, "Robert was an agent with DEA, as well. He's why I became an agent. He worked undercover in your town several years ago. Chester Carter had him killed along with a witness he was bringing in. He was damn good at his job, but his supervisor was dirty and betrayed him. He is why my father fights so hard for the crime bills in Congress, not for political gain. If it came down to family or politics, family would win every time. Don't ever think you and Abby are not the most important thing to me or even to my family. Abby is my parents' first grandchild, and they want to know her. It has killed them having to wait all this time to meet both of you."

"What about Brandi? Heather said she saw you meeting her on the street, and you obviously knew her that day at my dad's garage. Where does she fit into everything?"

He sighed and seemed to contemplate his answer. "I could get in a lot of trouble for telling you this. It goes against protocol and places her life at risk if word ever got out." He stared at me intently, the gravity of the situation clear in the tone of his voice.

"Brandi worked for Chase at his strip club on the highway, outside of town. He was so obsessed with you that anyone who displayed the slightest threat to you emotionally or physically, or who threatened his chances with you, he went after with a vengeance. He knew of the animosity between you two and targeted her because of it. He made Scott Wilson fire her on the trumped up charge of stealing from the register, ensuring no one else would hire her. She thought Chase would help her out with a job due to their past relationship, which he did as a waitress in his club. Only that wasn't enough. He threatened her parents, forcing her into stripping and prostitution." Gabe took a deep breath and blew it out before continuing.

"I spent time at the club trying to get any evidence I could on his operation or to have him draw me into his organization. When he found out I was seeing you, he ordered Brandi to try to seduce me. Chase promised her if she made it look like I cheated on you, he wouldn't make her prostitute herself any longer, only he didn't keep that promise. I think finding out you were pregnant with my baby sent him over the edge. He blamed her and as punishment, had her beaten and raped by several of his men."

My hands flew to my mouth in horror. No wonder she hated me so much when I saw her. "Gabe, no. Oh, my, God!" I closed my eyes and shook my head. I had been married to a true monster. What kind of man would blame an innocent person for my ending up pregnant? His hands cupped my face.

"Karsyn, don't do this to yourself. Do not blame yourself for his actions," he demanded. "Chase's crimes are his own. You didn't know, and you had nothing to do with it."

I opened my eyes and saw the worry on his face. I nodded I was okay for him to continue. "Is she okay? Is she safe? I may not have liked her, but I would never wish that on anyone."

"Physically she's fine, and she's getting counseling to help her cope with everything she's been through. She came to me a month after you got back. She figured out the baby you carried was mine and not Chase's. She'd learned enough from Chase and his men to realize I was more than a mechanic. She became a snitch for us, feeding us any information she could, but she didn't know a whole lot. After she confronted you that day with Abby, Chase beat her himself so badly, she spent over a week in the hospital. We knew it was only a matter of time before he killed her, so we pulled her out. She's in WITSEC, and she's getting a fresh start on life."

"Do you—" I paused, not sure I wanted an answer to my question. I was appalled at everything Chase had put her through, all because we didn't like each other, but I still felt that same old insecurity rise up inside me. "Do you see her often?" I asked hesitantly.

"No, Karsyn," he replied softly. "Her case is handled by another agent, now. I have no contact with her. I don't know where she is or what her new name is. She's safe and that's all that matters. She isn't my concern any longer. My only concern is you and Abby and keeping you safe. I love you, Karsyn. I have since that first day in the restaurant. You're the only one who has ever had my heart, and it's yours for as long as you want it."

"I love you, too," I whispered.

I swallowed the lump in my throat as the final pieces of my heart begin to heal. I had always been loved. I wasn't part of some master plan to do his job. He didn't use me. He wanted me for me even now after everything I'd done and everything we'd been through. I clung to him and felt all the fear and tension of the past melt away. I was finally where I belonged. His lips crushed mine, and I opened myself to him, welcoming him home. My hands went to his hair, remembering again the soft texture my fingers had missed. His fingers rushed through my hair to hold my head lovingly as he slowed our kiss before pulling away. His eyes stared into mine with so much love and passion.

"God, baby, I love you so much. I was so afraid when I got home and you weren't there. I drove my team relentlessly so we could wrap things up and I could get home to you. I couldn't wait to be with you and Abby. I stopped on the way to get a tree for our house. It's still on the porch at home, so we can put it up tomorrow together. I wanted to be here to spend Christmas together as a family."

"Home?" I asked, confused again. I pulled back to look up at him. "So it's not just another safe house? It's actually your home?" I stressed. I felt the beginnings of hope for all the dreams I'd allowed myself to entertain over the past few months, the dreams of a family, of safety, of love and peace.

He sighed and tilted his head, so his forehead rested against mine for a moment before pulling back. He guided me to the small leather loveseat and pulled me down beside him. He stared down at our hands, seeming to choose his words carefully.

"It's our home, or rather, it will be our home when you answer a question for me." He rubbed his face and suddenly seemed very nervous about what he wanted to say. "Do you remember when you were sick that Christmas after we fought? I told you I wanted to talk to you about something important?"

I nodded. "It was the day I found out I was pregnant with Abby and found you in bed with Brandi." There was no accusation in my voice. I knew the truth now; there was no reason to feel anything but sorrow for the turn my life had taken that night.

"When I left town, I went to my boss and convinced them to let me tell you the truth. That night we fought, proved how easily Chase could get to you, and I couldn't let that happen again. I couldn't convince you to stay away from him without giving you the reasons why and telling you who I really was. But it was for more than your safety. I had to be able to tell you the truth, so I would have the right to ask you something."

I stared at him in confusion as he pulled away from me. He slid off the seat to kneel on the floor in front of me as he reached into his pocket and took out a small, black velvet box. My hands flew to my mouth, and my gaze flew to the ring he revealed as he opened the lid. I looked back to his face again and was already nodding my head as he spoke the words I'd dreamed of for so long.

"Karsyn Louise McKenna, I love you with all my heart. I love our precious daughter whom we created in love. I promise to always love and protect you and our family until my dying day. I'll never lie to you or hide anything from you ever again. You're my life, my heart, and my soul. Please say you'll marry me."

"You promise there are no more secrets? Nothing else I need to know about? No ex-wives or other children?" I asked, only half joking.

He smiled and shook his head. "No Karsyn. Nothing else. Ever. It's just you, me, Abby, and whatever other children we're blessed with. There will never be another lie or secret between us, I swear to you. I love you. So what do you say? Will you?" he asked.

"Yes!" I cried as I threw my arms around him. I was laughing and crying as he slid the large diamond ring on my finger.

"She said, „yes!' She said, „yes!'" his sister shouted from the door.

We broke away laughing as the doors slid open, and Gabe's family surrounded us, offering congratulations. The butler came in and passed around champagne glasses as the senator proposed a toast to our future.

As I sipped my champagne, I remembered my concern from this morning and paused, turning to Gabe.

"Don't Abby and I have to go into Witness Protection soon? Will you be coming with us? How would that even work with your job?"

"Karsyn, do you understand what WITSEC is designed to do?" Senator Wingate asked before Gabe could answer.

"It's to protect us from anyone working for Chase's organization. Right?" My brow furrowed in confusion at his question.

I turned to Gabe for confirmation only to find a smile of indulgence on his face. It sort of pissed me off. Here I was trying to figure out how we could have a life together if Abby and I were going to be living somewhere in hiding under false identities. Did he think he'd just drop in on occasion to play house before he went back to the real world? I don't think so. He must have sensed my rising irritation because he quickly pulled me into his arms and kissed my forehead.

"Karsyn, baby, you're marrying into one of the most powerful, influential, political families of our time. My father is probably going to be the next president. You're marrying a federal agent. Why do you think I moved you to our home instead of another safe house? The neighborhood we live in is full of politicians and their families. There are so many Secret Service agents surrounding our family and our home. There's nowhere safer for you and our daughter than right here. I'm your protection. I meant what I said when I told you I would always keep you safe."

Epilogue

November 6, 2012

My eyes opened, and I turned my head to find the voice that woke me. I smiled as I spied him pacing in the corner, the small bundle held so carefully in his arms. He saw me watching him as he turned again and came over to sit on the side of the bed.

"How are you feeling? Are you in pain? Do you want me to call the nurse?" he whispered.

"No, I'm okay. Just tired and sore. Does he need to be changed?" I asked as I reached to pull down the edge of the blanket in his arms. I smiled at the sight of the tuft of black hair. He was beautiful.

"I already did it. A nurse came in a little earlier to help me. I didn't want to wake you. You had a long night and needed to rest." He carefully leaned over and gave me a gentle kiss as he placed our son in my arms. I smiled and stared down in wonder at our newest creation and couldn't resist brushing my fingers over his cheek as his small mouth searched before latching onto my breast to nurse. He was beautiful and perfect with his ten tiny fingers and ten tiny toes.

"I'm still upset with you, Karsyn. Why didn't you say something sooner? We didn't have to go tonight. You scared me, baby. What if something went wrong and I had lost you tonight?"

"I'm sorry you were worried. I honestly thought I would have more time, and I wanted to be there to show our support for your father. It was his big night, and he wanted his family with him. I'm so sorry I ruined it. Do you think he'll ever forgive me?"

The heat rose in my face as I remembered my mortification. I mean, how often does someone have her water break while an entire nation watched? Our son, deciding to steal the limelight, interrupted what was the most important event in his grandfather's life, giving his acceptance speech after winning the presidential election.

I had been feeling discomfort and small twinges all day but assumed they were Braxton Hicks since it was still two weeks from my due date. By the time I realized I was in actual labor, we were already standing on stage with his family, listening to his father's speech. I had been discreetly watching the timing of my contractions, but Gabe caught me looking at my watch one too many times and noticed the color drain from my face as water suddenly pooled at my feet.

I delivered our son in the back of the ambulance. We didn't even make it out of the parking lot. Fortunately, everything went smoothly, and at 10:34 p.m. on Election Day, Jackson Carson Wingate was born.

Gabe laughed softly at me and kissed my head. "Finish feeding my son and don't worry about my dad. He's just happy you're both alright."

When I finished nursing, he lifted Jackson to his chest to burp and turned at the sound of a quiet knock on the door before it opened. The first thing I saw was the familiar faces of the Secret Service agents who surrounded my in-laws. After a brief nod from Gabe that the room was secure, they stepped back and allowed Gabe's parents to enter, followed by his sister, brother, and sister-in-law.

I shook my head in wonder. Sometimes it still threw me how different my life was. Agents always surrounded us, either in the line of duty or in the line for dinner. When you're married to an agent and your father-in-law is running for office, you find your friends in the wives of other agents or politicians. Gabe had been right; there wasn't a safer environment for us than by his side. There had only been one attempt on my life early on, and that was quickly squashed. Gabe didn't even know I was aware of it. He worked so hard to give us a normal life that he didn't want me to worry. To keep him happy, I pretend I didn't know about it, but I diligently followed every precaution he had set out for us so it would never happen again.

I smiled at the sight of Daniel coming in the room, carrying Abby, who slept on his shoulder clutching her doll. To the rest of the world, he was the President. To Abby, he was just Papa, and he spoiled her rotten. Cecile went straight to Gabe to take Jackson from him, cooing at him as she finished rocking him to sleep. Katherine and Lana each kissed my cheek before going over to sit next to Cecile on the window seat, cooing also. Lana absently rubbed her own baby bump. She and Richard are expecting their first in a few months.

Gabe tried to take Abby from his father.

"No, Daddy. Papa said I get to spend the night," she protested sleepily as she clung tighter to his father.

It still filled my heart to hear Abby call Gabe Daddy, and I know it did the same for him. We were fortunate Abby was so young when everything happened. It took a couple of months for Abby to warm up to him, but by the time we married the following summer, Chase was forgotten, a distant memory, and she was calling Gabe Daddy. He was her favorite person in the world, next to her dog, Risk.

"That's right, Sweetpea, but don't you want to kiss Momma goodnight and see your new baby brother?"

Her head popped up at the news, and she leaned over so Gabe could take her. "Jack's here? He can't play with my doll because she only loves me, but I'll teach him how to throw the ball to Risk."

"It'll be a while before he's big enough to throw balls," Gabe said with a chuckle. "He's just a baby right now."

Gabe took her to his mother, and Abby leaned in to kiss Jack's cheek. She introduced her doll, Maddy, to him and laid down the rules that he couldn't touch her. I smiled as she explained if he was good, Pops would get him his own doll. Pops had become a good friend to us over the years. He resigned from the DEA six months after our ordeal and now worked as part of Daniel's security detail. I think he just couldn't stand the idea of not seeing Abby again. His youngest daughter was one of my best friends. He treated me as if I was one of his own, helping to fill the void left by my dad's death and loved Abby like his own granddaughter.

I turned my attention to Daniel, who had come over to me. I smiled at him as he sat in the chair beside me.

"He's a handsome boy, Karsyn. You and Gabe did good, but I have a bone to pick with you, young lady," he said sternly. I bit my bottom lip to stop the grin, which threatened, as his persona changed from Daniel the family man to Daniel the President and most powerful man in the nation. "What were you thinking coming tonight if you were in labor? You shouldn't have put yourself or my grandson in that position. You had us all worried about you."

"I'm sorry, Daniel. Tonight was your night, and I knew how important it was for everyone to be there for you. I'm sorry I ruined it for you."

His eyebrows rose at my comment. "Ruined it for me? Karsyn Louise Wingate, I don't give a damn about my speech. No one really cares one way or another about what I had to say tonight. I promise you, probably seventy-five percent of the population is glad it's over and their normal TV programs won't be interrupted for another three years. They only care that I do the job I promised to do. My concern is you and my grandson. You put yourselves in a bad situation tonight for no good reason. Don't do it again," he ordered.

I let go of the grin I was holding in and saluted him. "Yes, sir, Mr. President."

He narrowed his eyes at me and shook his head, chuckling. "You scared the hell out of everyone tonight. Secret Service plans for every contingency: terrorists, fanatics, disgruntled voters. You name it, they're prepared." He lifted his hand in the air with one finger raised. "Everything, that is, except pregnant daughter-in-laws. You single-handedly brought the Secret Service, CIA, and FBI to their knees tonight. They should have known better. You, young lady, are a dangerous woman."

Everyone in the room was laughing at his comments except the agents in charge of his protection. I could tell by the disgruntled looks on their faces that I would be doing a lot of baking in the near future to make it up to them—except for Pops. He gave me a knowing wink and smiled.

Everyone left shortly after, and I was alone again with my husband and new baby. I thought about my life and the paths I had chosen that all led me to this place. I still wished things had happened differently. I missed Heather and not a day went by that I didn't think of my dad and wished he was here.

My hand absently reached for my locket, and I opened the clasp. I smiled at the family picture inside of Gabe, Abby, and I. It would be replaced again in a couple of months, now that Jackson was here. I looked at the picture of my parents and raised my locket to my lips.

"I love you, Daddy, and I miss you. You'd be proud of me. I'm living life with both eyes open."

LaVergne, TN USA
27 October 2010
202506LV00002B/4/P